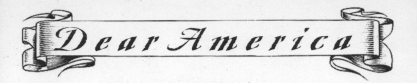

Dear America

A Time For Courage

The Diary of Kathleen Bowen

by Kathryn Lasky

Scholastic Inc. New York

WASHINGTON, D.C.
1917

WASHINGTON, D.C.
JANUARY 1, 1917

Mother gave me this diary for Christmas, but I am really
not quite sure what to write in it. I mean, my life seems
so dull compared with others. Everyone else has a mission in the world, or if not a mission there is the Great
War raging now in Europe. Mother and Auntie Claire
have their National Woman's Party, which keeps them
busy all hours of the day, much to Uncle Bayard's disgust
and my own father's worry. Nell, my oldest sister, has
also joined the Woman's Party. She is the official press
secretary. She gets to meet with all the newspaper people
and tell them what Alice Paul, the president of the party,
is up to. Now, if I were a seventeen- or eighteen-year-old
boy, I suppose I would be worrying about America entering the Great War. I might be having soldier dreams of
glory and nonfatal wounds, but wounds big enough and
in the right place so that the scars are visible — nothing
badly disfiguring, just dashing. Oh, yes, I hear these boys
talking, especially my cousin Henry and his friends.

But I'm just me — Kathleen Bowen, "Kat" for short, thirteen years old, eighth grade in Miss Pruitt's Academy for Young Ladies at Fifteenth and L Streets, Washington, D.C., a short walk from my own front door. Alma Minette, born on the same day within the same hour — most extraordinary — is not only my cousin, but also my best friend. Even though we're cousins we don't look a thing alike. Alma is very tall and everyone always thinks she is older than me, which can be annoying, except she is so nice. Whereas I have mousey brown hair, Alma has pale red hair. And her face is just more grown-up. But Alma thinks her life is just as uneventful and boring as mine. She goes to Miss Pruitt's too. Our school is supposed to be very advanced and modern, with a curriculum similar to the one given boys — Latin, geometry, drawing, and not just watercolor and arty things but architectural drafting, that is my favorite course. But my life is still pretty boring. Every afternoon when school lets out, Alma and I walk partway home together. We stop at the Ardmore, a drugstore with a soda fountain, and we sit on high stools and drink ice-cream sodas. Well, not always sodas. In the early fall and late spring and summer when it is warm we have lime rickeys — lime juice and fizzy water with sweet syrup.

In what we call the bumper season, when it is not quite winter or not yet spring, we have ice-cream sodas. In winter, we have hot chocolate with mountains of whipped cream. And then sometimes for a special occasion we share a banana split.

JANUARY 2, 1917

Something exciting has happened. I am going to get to meet The Mosquito, the one who buzzes in President Wilson's ear — Miss Alice Paul herself, who started the Woman's Party that Mother and Auntie Claire belong to. There is to be a meeting at our house in two nights.

The meeting is to discuss something called the "deputation." It is a fancy word for going to the White House to see the president, President Woodrow Wilson. The Woman's Party wants to demand women's suffrage, the right for women to vote. President Wilson is very slippery about all this. He often says he agrees with them but he does nothing. In any case Mother has asked Alma and me to help serve the tea and cakes. Rumor has it that President Wilson said that Alice Paul was worse than a thorn in his side, that she was a bloodsucking mosquito in his ear, because unlike a thorn she makes an incessant noise that could drive a victim mad while sticking one for blood. Mother is worried that Uncle Bayard might not permit Auntie Claire to come. Uncle Bayard is the stubbornest man on Earth. Even Father says so.

LATER

I didn't mean to be eavesdropping, but I heard Father on the telephone in his study. The door was partway open and he was talking to Uncle Bayard. He was saying, "Bayard, it is better that they have this meeting here right under our own noses than go off someplace. At least we can keep an eye on things." I knew he was trying to persuade Uncle Bayard to let Auntie Claire come for the meeting. I am not sure, however, if Mother would have approved of his argument. Just as he was saying this, Nell came up, so she heard him too and actually stuck her tongue out at the door when he said the part about "keeping an eye on them." Nobody better ever try to keep an eye on Nell. Several boyfriends have made attempts — no use at all. She gets rid of any beau who tries to tell her what to do or breathes a word of marriage. Cassie, my next oldest sister, who goes to Radcliffe College in Cambridge, Massachusetts, thinks a lot about getting married.

JANUARY 3, 1917

Uncle Bayard will not let Auntie Claire come for the meeting and of course he won't let Alma come. I found out today in school. Alma was late and her face seemed very puffy and her eyes all red. She slipped me a note in Latin — I mean, of course, in Latin class, not written in Latin. Hah! What a joke! We just began our term of Latin a few weeks ago and all we know how to say is *ego sum puella* (I am a girl), *ego sum argentarius* (I am a banker), *ego sum nauta* (I am a sailor), and then I know how to say a few things about this fellow, Caecilius, in our Latin book such as "Caecilius is not in his villa and he is in the forum."

But anyway, Alma seemed awfully upset. Then Uncle Bayard sent his chauffeur to school early to pick up Alma so we barely got a chance to talk at all. And that is really too bad because just yesterday we said that it has been ages since we have had a banana split at the Ardmore, and we were planning to today. I would hate living in Alma's house. There are eight children but it seems like millions. Every year Auntie Claire has a new one. And Uncle Bayard is so stern. Most of the children are boys except for Alma and Clarice. But Clarice, or Clary, has something wrong with her brain so even though she is five years older than Alma she can't speak very well and she doesn't know how to read or write. She is like a very quiet five-year-old. It's very sad, for there is no companionship for Alma. There are two older brothers, Henry and Bayard. Bayard is just like his father — thinks himself quite swell. I even once heard Auntie Claire say that young Bayard was born middle-aged. Henry is disgusting in the way so many teenage boys are. Then there are just rafts of little boys younger than Alma — Gerald, Beauregard, Halsey, and Davis.

January 4, 1917

Well, I met her! Met Alice Paul. She is not at all like a mosquito nor is she like the bossy general that the news-papers and all those who are against her and the

Woman's Party say. She is so much the opposite of everything I expected. I mean, Alice Paul, this woman of action who has led marches and confronted congressmen and senators, well, what I shall always most remember about her is her utter stillness. She is almost without motion, even when she does move. She is the calmest, loveliest creature. Not a bit unwomanly or mannish as the papers often say. She is slender and delicate with an utterly peaceful face framed with wavy brown hair. There is a cunning dimple in her chin that gives her an almost playful look, until you look at her eyes, which are large and gray and very serious. But it is the stillness of her that most impresses. It is not the stillness of a statue nor one of a dead person — hardly! She is most alive. Mother calls it a Quaker stillness, for Quakers are much at peace within themselves, she says, and resolute in their beliefs, and Alice Paul is a Quaker.

I helped Marietta, our colored maid, serve the tea and Marietta let me pass the cakes. When I brought one to Miss Paul she asked me my name and age and what I was studying. She seemed pleased about the Latin and drafting. She said she hoped they would begin to introduce life sciences.

When the meeting began I was supposed to go to bed,

but I came out again in my wrapper and sat in the shadowy curve of our staircase where I can see everything but not be seen. The women talked about what they would do if (1) President Wilson refused to see them and (2) if he saw them but ignored their demand. There was much talk of a vigil and then something they called a picket line. I know what *vigil* means — from the Latin *viglia,* which means watchfulness. But a picket? Sounds like a fence to me.

JANUARY 5, 1917

There was an envelope waiting for me on the mail desk this morning. Mother said it was from Miss Paul. I opened it and there were two pieces of paper inside. The first was a note from Miss Paul saying, "Dear Kathleen, This is one of my favorite speeches ever made by a woman. I have copied it out for many friends and young girls. It was given by a woman named Sojourner Truth, who was once a slave. She could not read or write but she had a keen mind." Here I am copying it out in my diary because when I read the words they made something stir inside me. They are words that go very deep even though my life has been very different from Miss Truth's.

"That man over there say that women need to be helped into carriages, and lifted over ditches and to have the best place everywhere. Nobody ever helps me into carriages, or over mud puddles, or gives me any best place and ain't I a woman? Look at me! Look at my arm! I have ploughed and planted and gathered into barns and no man could head me — and ain't I a woman? I could work as much and eat as much as a man — when I could get it — and bear the lash as well! And ain't I a woman? I have borne thirteen children, and seen most all sold off to slavery, and when I cried out with my mother's grief, none but Jesus heard me — and ain't I a woman?"

JANUARY 6, 1917

Oh, dear, I am so worried about Alma. You can't imagine what happened this morning. Marietta came knocking on my door early. And it's a Saturday at that! She had a piece of paper in her hand. She said Juby had brought it. Juby is Marietta's sister and is one of the maids in Alma's house. I opened the note and read it, my hands trembling.

"Please, please invite me over to spend the night. I can't face another night of this awfulness between Mother and Father. The boys are all on Father's side and Clary just wanders around clutching her dolly and smiling. I have no one — Alma"

Alma didn't need to say it, but I knew I would have to think up a good reason for her to come, something her father would approve, and certainly not serving tea to Alice Paul and the Woman's Party.

Marietta broke in. She must have been reading my thoughts and she must have read the note. "Tell her she got to come over tonight 'cause I got that cambric for your summer tea dresses and we've got to fit them up tonight." I looked up, stunned at Marietta's words. A big wide smile cracked her cinnamon-colored face. "I ain't stupid. After all, Juby tells me plenty and I know that sometimes Mr. Minette act bad, but I don't believe he is bad."

"My father doesn't act bad," I said, "and I know he doesn't like all this Women's Party stuff."

"Your father, Dr. Bowen, is a gol-darned saint. He's good to all women. You have to be when you delivers their babies and such."

"Not necessarily. Father says Dr. Rhinitz is a mean old cantankerous man who should not be let near a woman or child."

Well, then Marietta and I argued some more. We are famous for our arguments — discussions, really. Mother says that I distract Marietta from her work and that Marietta distracts me from my studies. I happen to like it this way. Half the things Marietta does for me I can do myself, so why shouldn't I go ahead and do them so we get more time to talk? It's just when she stops her vacuuming and dusting that Mother really frets.

JANUARY 7, 1917

Sunday nights are so dreadful. I am behind in my Latin translation and have two more math problems, and then I am supposed to choose an Emily Dickinson poem and write a short essay about it. I am going to choose a short poem. Of course, Alma and I should have been doing homework, but we were having so much fun there wasn't time. I mean, the whole point, after all, was for Alma to get some relief from that house of hers with screaming children, angry adults, and arrogant older brothers.

It was actually Mother who interrupted us just as we were, well, not exactly starting our homework, but considering it. Mother came in with a whole pile of white, gold, and purple fabric and asked if we could deliver it over to Mrs. O. H. P. Belmont's apartments. She lives in New York but keeps large apartments here, not far from us. We are at K and Seventeenth streets and Mrs. Belmont's is just off K near Franklin Park. Mrs. Belmont is VERY rich and VERY grand and she is one of the most important people in the Woman's Party. Because of her money and how smart she is, she has become one of the most important people in the suffrage movement. She gave the money to buy the building for the headquarters of the Woman's Party on Lafayette Square directly across from the White House. There were many other buildings they could have bought, but when the one on Lafayette Square came up she said, "That's it. We'll be right there all the time. The first thing President Wilson sees in the morning when he wakes up, the last thing when he goes to bed." I am not sure whether this is absolutely true because I don't know if Mrs. Belmont really knows where the president's bedroom is, but nonetheless there is little escaping the Woman's Party when it is right across the street.

When we delivered the cloth we were ushered into an elaborate parlor and then we heard a soft rustling. It was Mrs. Belmont's taffeta afternoon gown. She is a large woman and the fabric for her gown was — well, a lot, so you could hear her before you could see her. She swept into the room like a ship. She reminds me so much of a ship because she has a large, firm bosom that precedes her like the prow of a vessel. Her eyes were merry and she thanked us for "helping the cause." When I introduced Alma a shadow passed across her eyes. "Better not tell your father you've been here."

Alma blushed that insane fiery shade she gets. With her red hair she looks like a haystack on fire. "Oh, don't worry, dear. We're working on him and he is not the only one, you know. I have quite a touch with these men. You know, they are so silly when a very rich woman tells them something. This is one of the best parts about having money."

Went to the Ardmore on the way home. Not in a banana-split mood. We had chocolate ice-cream sodas.

Alma went to church with us in the morning. Then we took her back home. She gave me a squeeze and a kiss as she stepped off the running board of the Hudson. "You saved me. I can face them now." Then she dashed into the house. I cannot say I felt exactly good. I am just not sure why things have to be this way. Wouldn't it be wonderful if Alma could be Mrs. Belmont's daughter? No! That wouldn't be right. I love Auntie Claire and Auntie Claire loves Alma. Oh, this is so hard.

JANUARY 8, 1917

I love the smell of ironing. There is something so cozy and warm about it. I went down to the basement where Marietta irons after school and took some of the leftover cake from the meeting. Marietta and I had an interesting discussion. I was thinking about what Mrs. Belmont had said about having money. It was rather shocking. I said, "Marietta, do you think it is polite to talk about having lots of money?"

She said, "I wouldn't have an opinion on that."

I said, "Why not?"

She put down the iron on its back heel and peered at me with those pale brown eyes of hers like I was the dumbest thing in the world. "'Cuz I doan have no money, so why should I have an opinion about talking about it or not?"

"But you must have thought about having money," I persisted.

"Yeah, but if I did I wouldn't be thinkin' 'bout talkin' about it. I'd be thinkin' about spendin' it."

"You should be thinking about investing it." Thus, another argument between me and Marietta was beginning.

She stopped ironing and looked up at me again. Her bottom lip poked way out. "You tryin' to tell me how to spend the money I doan have? Well, that takes the cake, Kat."

"I am not trying to tell you. I am just giving you financial advice."

She rolled her eyes toward the ceiling and then picked up the sprinkle can and wetted down the shirt she was ironing. There was a hiss as the iron hit the sleeve. "Where'd you become such an expert?"

"Uncle Bayard is a great financier."

"I heard." Marietta muttered, "Dat's about the only thing he's great at. Aside from gettin' children on your poor aunt."

"How come Auntie has had so many babies and Mama has had only Nell, Cassie, and me?"

Now Marietta rolled her lower lip back in until her

mouth pressed together into a thin crease. She looked at me hard. "Now, you git this straight, Kat. I am hired to do the ironing and the laundry, and now the cookin' since Pearl's been sick. I do the vacuuming and the dusting and I serve at your parents' dinner parties, but I do NOT explain to you about babies and life."

She is, of course, dead wrong. Most of the interesting things I have learned about life I've learned from Marietta, or her sister Juby, or Juby's husband, Joss. They might not know it but I listen and I hear them talk. Learned about how if you wrap a cut with cobwebs it can stop the bleeding. I asked Father about it and he said he had heard that was what old colored folks often did but that he wasn't going to try it in surgery. I thought I might try it if I get a paper cut sometime or just a hangnail. In any case I have learned a lot from Marietta and none of it is one speck boring, unlike Miss Pruitt's Academy.

JANUARY 9, 1917

Mother is as mad as I have ever seen her. She came back from that deput-what thing at the White House and she said — well, I couldn't believe it — my mother said one word under her breath about the president that I think I would have been spanked for saying. She called President Wilson as dumb as — I shall write it here very small — A HORSE'S BEHIND. I cannot believe my very own mother said those words. I simply cannot believe it! And to think I thought there would be nothing interesting to write about. Who needs a mission? Who needs a Great War? My mother said BEHIND — and she called the president a horse's you-know-what.

Father was so alarmed, he offered her a glass of sherry. Mother shrieked, "Don't offer me a glass of sherry! I am angry and with good reason! That foolish president. To think that he thinks he can so lightly dismiss us and say that he must defer to his party. What in heaven's name has the Democratic Party ever done for women? And never has a Democratic Party leader had more power than Mr. Wilson. To use these facile arguments on us! How simple does he think we are?"

And then once more she muttered The Word. This is

just amazing. As Miss Pruitt says, life can be a wonderful and mysterious thing. She was talking about caterpillars turning into butterflies, and I am talking about . . . oh, it is too funny. My mother!

LATER

When Nell got home I couldn't wait to tell her. And she just scowled at me. "Do you think that is all that happened today? That mother said a justifiably rotten word about our rotten president? Is that all this means to you?" I didn't know what to answer. I had never seen so many angry women in one house. "Well, tomorrow you'll find out."

"What do you mean?" I asked. Then all of Nell's anger seemed to fade and she grabbed both my hands in hers. Her dark brown hair curled around her face. Her dark eyes flashed. "Oh, Kat, it is all so exciting. Do you realize we raised three thousand dollars within two hours of leaving the White House?"

"Mrs. Belmont?"

"No, others. And tomorrow the picket line starts."

"What's a picket line?" I asked.

Nell rolled her eyes in disbelief. "Wait and see!" Then she ran out of my bedroom.

JANUARY 14, 1917

I cannot believe that I once did not know what a picket line was. Well, I certainly know now. It is all we eat, think, and breathe — the White House vigil, the picket line. And all that white, gold, and purple cloth Alma and I delivered to Mrs. Belmont's, well, our fingers are just about worn out from sewing banners for the pickets to carry. Alma helps too. We tell her father that we are staying after school for Latin Club or the drawing and painting circle. Yes, it's a lie. But Alma and I say no one is getting hurt by our lie and then we go over to the Woman's Party headquarters on Lafayette Square and help make banners. They need a steady supply for the women in the picket line. And Alma's mother is in it! Alma said that her mother threatened to tell our Uncle Everett, Mother's and Auntie Claire's brother, about a gold mining venture that she thinks is bad but that Uncle

Bayard wants Uncle Everett up in Boston to invest in. It worked, and Auntie Claire and Mother are standing by the White House gates with a dozen or more other women, holding banners that read, THE RIGHT OF SELF-GOVERNMENT FOR ONE-HALF OF ITS PEOPLE IS OF FAR MORE VITAL CONSEQUENCE TO THE NATION THAN ANY OR ALL OTHER QUESTIONS or MR. PRESIDENT, WHAT WILL YOU DO FOR WOMEN'S SUFFRAGE?, or my favorite, MEN, THEIR RIGHTS AND NOTHING MORE; WOMEN, THEIR RIGHTS AND NOTHING LESS.

The weather is bitter cold, close to zero. Everyone expected the women to quit after the first day. The newspaper photographers came and took a few pictures. But the women, including Mother and Auntie Claire and Nell, have been coming back for four days, even today, Sunday. The newspapers who at first referred to them simply as "women participants in a vigil for suffrage" are now calling them "unwomanly and undesirable."

Alma and I bring them hot bricks wrapped in toweling to stand on to keep their feet warm. Father is endlessly fretting about Mother and Auntie Claire getting pneumonia, "or worse." He sent Marietta over with thermoses of hot soup that Mother, Nell, and Auntie Claire shared with the other women. Alma and I went to the

Ardmore and had hot chocolate with piles of whipped cream.

By the way, Nell thinks Cassie should come home from Radcliffe to join the picket line, but even Mother is against this.

JANUARY 18, 1917

The picket line has been going on for more than a week! And people said they would not last a day and the weather still has not broken. What's more, news of the pickets is spreading and more and more women are coming from other parts of the district and some from as far away as Maryland and Virginia. President Wilson felt so sorry for them in the cold that he invited them in for coffee but they refused. They said they would come in only to talk about a federal amendment for the women's right to vote. No coffee! This made me think of Sojourner Truth's words about men who help lift women into carriages and over mud puddles — that, of course, is the easy part, just like giving them coffee. Giving them the vote is the hard part.

JANUARY 19, 1917

These days are a little strange. If Father has an emergency or has to go deliver a baby I am often the only one at the dinner table, because Mother and Nell take the late afternoon shift on the picket line. And when Father is there, he and I really don't have that much to talk about because for some reason all is dwarfed by the picket line or yes, the Great War. There is some talk about America entering it, so it is difficult to talk about other things. I mean, Father tries. But the words seem to fall into deep empty spaces, for there is something so insignificant about the usual school-type chitchat: "Kat, tell me how it goes with Latin. Just wait until you get to Virgil — you'll love Virgil."

But I am still in the *hortō* (garden) or the *culinā* (kitchen) with Caecillius's wife or in the *forō* (forum) with Caecillius himself. This evening at dinner we talked about geometry a bit and then about summer. Summer seems so far away. I wonder if the picket line will still be going in the summer. Or will we be in the war?

Oh, Lord, I just had a terrible thought! What if America goes into the war and Father must go too because he is a doctor and Mother is still on the picket line?

And Nell says that if America gets into the war she is going to join the Women's Ambulance Corps. She doesn't even know how to drive! But the point is I shall be left all alone. It is a chilling thought. Imagine me sitting by myself in the big dining room night after night with only Marietta bringing in covered dishes of steamed vegetables and plates of ham and corn bread just for me. I thought the clinking of our spoons in the soup bowl made such a lonely noise tonight in the dim winter light of the dining room. Imagine the sound of one spoon and me occasionally smacking my lips. That is absolutely pathetic. I don't mean to sound selfish, but I don't think I should be orphaned even for a noble cause.

JANUARY 20, 1917

Still worried about being orphaned. Alma says I am a fool. She said she would come over and have dinner with me and lend me some of her baby brothers — thanks, but no thanks. We made two new banners today. Alma said she thinks Uncle Bayard has either given up on her mother or is very worried about business or both. He goes to New York a lot.

January 21, 1917

I happened to mention to Father that Uncle Bayard was in New York and he raised his eyebrow way high up the way he does when something is perplexing him. "Oh, really!" he said, and I said, "How come you're raising your eyebrow so high up just about Uncle Bayard going to New York?"

The eyebrow came right down and Father gave me a sharp look as if I had caught him at something. "Nothing. Nothing," he said quickly, which I knew really meant that something was going on. Then he said, "Why did you ask?"

"Ask about what?" I said.

He coughed a little. "My eyebrow."

"Oh, nothing. Nothing," I replied right back. We both knew we were lying, but I don't want him to know that I might know about Uncle Bayard's business problems with the gold mine. Children are not supposed to know stuff like that.

I think people lie a lot, not really to deceive or mislead, just to get over the rough spots. There are a lot of rough spots these days. I know that Father is very worried about Mother. I know he really does not think she should be out there every day for such long hours in the cold. I know he thinks women's suffrage is probably a nice thing but wishes women had never had the idea. But he never really says these things. I think people often lie for love.

JANUARY 22, 1917

President Wilson made a big speech today about the Great War and he spoke in favor of what he called "peace without victory," which means that all the countries who are fighting should get together and figure things out and he will help them. Now, why can't he sit down with Mother and Auntie Claire and Lucy Burns and Mrs. Stevens and Alice Paul, Harriet Stanton Blatch, and all these women who have been picketing for two weeks, and talk with them about voting? Just let them vote. This is so easy next to war.

JANUARY 23, 1917

I have been going nearly every day to take hot bricks and snacks and thermoses of coffee. I know nearly all the ladies in the picket line. They are all very nice. Some of them seem so frail, like Mrs. Stevens. She is as skinny as a stick and her nose turns bright red in the cold. She stands there hour in, hour out until her replacement comes, but she is always cheerful and seems so energetic.

The oddest thing is that not only have I come to know the women on the picket line but the White House police as well. They are very nice and very sympathetic to the women. Mother was asking Sergeant Reilly how the little one with the croup was and told him what Father always prescribes, and then the next day he told her how well that plaster from the pharmacy had worked and was most grateful. Then he added, with a twinkle in his eye, "I might never have learned it, Mrs. Bowen, had you not been here on the picket line asking for the vote."

"Ahh, yes, Sergeant Reilly. You see what happens when women get out into the world."

"You betcha!" He nodded cheerily.

JANUARY 24, 1917

Well, the Silent Sentinels, as the newspaper started out calling the women in the picket line, are now being called in the paper besides "unwomanly and undesirable," "dangerous," "unsexed," and "pathological," which I had to look up in a dictionary. It means "caused by or involving disease." So women are "diseased" if they want to vote. "That's a fine kettle of fish," as my Grandma Bowen used to say.

Everybody seems to think that the women should have "gotten over this" by now, as if it were a cold or something — that they should have gone home. But they haven't and new women come every day. Mother does not have to stand for quite as long, as there are three or four others willing to take her place. Representative Emerson from Ohio called the women's vigil an "insult to the president" and another congressman called them "iron-jawed angels." I think it is a stupid term for flesh-and-blood women who merely want the same right to vote as men.

JANUARY 25, 1917

Alma and I are making a list of all the mean, nasty words the newspapers use to describe women, and even some of them that are not so nasty but in many ways are just as bad.

Here they are:
NASTIES
freakish
unsexed
mannish
witches
succubuses on society (had to look up *succubus:* a
demon in female form, a she-devil)

NOT-SO-NASTIES
weak
silly
distractible
illogical
dependent
flighty

FEBRUARY 1, 1917

Shocking news! The Germans announced that they will
begin "unrestricted submarine warfare" immediately.
That means they plan to blow up any ship they want to
with their U-boats that sail under the water and shoot

missiles. This is very bad. Now everyone is talking war. Mother and Nell even came home early from the picket line. It was the first time in three weeks that we all had dinner together. Despite this it was a very quiet dinner. It was as if there was more unspoken than spoken. I had the feeling that everyone was having a private conversation with themselves. Father, I imagined, was thinking about treating the wounded. There is a terrible new weapon called mustard gas, and it blinds the soldiers and burns out their lungs or something horrible. So I bet he was thinking about that. And Mother, well, I am not sure what she was thinking, but this cannot help the vigil. Nell behaved very strangely. She had spots of bright color on her cheeks and seemed very nervous. But I think Nell was thinking about joining the ambulance corps. I am sure of it. And I was just thinking about Mother and Father and Nell and what they were thinking about and about becoming an orphan, more or less.

LATER

Hah! Told you so. I heard Nell asking Marietta if she could ask Juby's husband, Joss, who is the chauffeur for Alma's family, if he would teach her how to drive. We don't have a chauffeur and Nell would never dream of asking Father. That would give away her plans immediately.

February 2, 1917

Last night I went to Nell's room and told her outright that I knew her plans. She suddenly looked really scared. "Don't tell Mother."

"What about Father?" I asked. But it was Mother she was most concerned with. You see, the Woman's Party is against America entering the war. Alice Paul says, Why should Americans go and fight for democracy abroad when our president does not defend it at home? Nell doesn't quite agree. She feels that the Great War should be a separate cause from that of suffrage. She says there are actually other women in the party who feel this way too, but not Alice Paul and not Mother and not Auntie Claire. I am not sure what I think. It does seem rather silly to be going all across the ocean and having young men get killed for democracy, when there is a battle right here and those poor women are freezing their feet and getting sick. Mrs. Walter Evans collapsed this afternoon on the picket line with pneumonia and they say her condition is critical. Is she any less brave than a poor Brit blinded by mustard gas? Is her cause less noble? And I know that this is not very nice to say but what about Nell? Are her ambitions all that noble? Or is she also out looking for adventure and a chance to learn how to drive?

I, of course, am feeling very left out of everything. I am too young to be a silent sentinel and stand on the picket line. They allow you only if you are over twenty-one. And nobody cares what I think about the Great War, because why would anyone ever ask a thirteen-year-old girl? I am fit only to be an orphan. I shall start reading Charles Dickens, *Oliver Twist,* I guess.

FEBRUARY 3, 1917

Our country and Germany have officially stopped talking. President Wilson ordered it. And he has also asked for the power to arm all American merchant ships against German U-boats in case of attack. When Mother came home from her shift she said, "Well, we're like the Germans now, I suppose — for he hasn't talked to us since we started the vigil. I suppose next he shall ask for the power to take arms against us." I felt as if the breath had been sucked right out of me. As soon as she said it she clapped her hands over her mouth. Her eyes went wide at the horror of her own words. She raced across the parlor and folded me into her arms. She tried to comfort me. But I was stiff with fear.

LATER

Tonight I had not been asleep long when I heard my bedclothes rustle. It was Mother in her nightgown. She was crawling into bed beside me. She put her arms around me and whispered, "Poor Kat." Something burst inside me and I started sobbing. The whole bed shook. Mother just said, "There, there," and patted my head. I knew somehow she understood. I am so glad that she did not try to tell me how everyone had to sacrifice in these times or how noble the cause was. I am sick of noble causes. Good night.

February 4, 1917

Bitter cold this morning. When I woke up there were frost designs on my window. And when I looked down on Farragut Square, which is directly across from our house, it looked as if the statue of the admiral, Admiral Farragut, who won the Battle of New Orleans, had been dipped in ice. Everything is glazed — streets, lampposts, the black limbs of the trees. The sun is harsh and too bright, and its rays fracture into tiny brilliant slivers as they hit the ice-sheathed street. A mean wind from the north creaks around the eaves of our house. When I was looking out the window, I saw this tiny figure moving down the street, hunched against the slicing wind, stepping carefully so as not to lose footing. It was Mother! I looked back at my bed. There was still a hollow in the pillow where her head had rested near mine. I don't know when she left my bed this morning, or maybe it was last night. I felt a twinge of shame that I was relieved that she did not speak to me of noble causes. She need not speak. Look how she bends herself into the wind. She is like a small sailing vessel in a vast and stormy sea as she sets her course for the White House to stand sentinel.

I suppose the Wilsons are having their morning coffee. And maybe some fancy breakfast rolls. They say there is a very good pastry chef in the White House. I wonder what Mrs. Wilson thinks when she sees these women standing out there, bundled against the cold, their faces wrapped with woolen scarves against the wind. I wonder what they talk about to each other. How could the Wilsons completely ignore the women? Have these people no feelings? How could you as a woman be married to somebody like him — President Wilson? It is not simply that he is against the vote. It is that he can make so small of their cause, that he can go on in his comfort, eating while the women are cold. I think the first requirement to be president should be that the person is human, and the First Lady should be also. I would never sit there stuffing my mouth with pastry as good women freeze outside for their natural rights.

LATER

Made five trips to the picket lines today to deliver hot wrapped bricks and thermoses of coffee. Father joined me on one but then got an emergency call from the hospital. I found Alma at my house with Clary when I got back from the third trip and they accompanied me. I think it was good for Clary to go with us and take a brick. She has a hard time understanding what her mother is doing. Auntie Claire was so thrilled to see Clary and Clary to see Auntie Claire, for often Clary is asleep or with her special tutor at the school she goes to when Auntie Claire returns. They hugged and whooped. Their heads were swallowed up in a cloud of fog from their breath and hollering. It was so cold that their eyes were watering and then they began to cry. Halfway home I noticed two tear tracks had frozen on Clary's cheeks. We brought her inside my house and showed her. She laughed and when I started to dab them off with a warm towel she said, "No! No!" Then she cried and the new warm tears melted the frozen ones. It was so sad, because she was trying to catch them and keep them like one would a souvenir for a scrapbook. We made her some hot chocolate and I got down my old Mother Goose, which she always seems to like, and began reading her some verses. She seemed fine by the time they left. Of course, we had to give her many instructions about not telling her father where she had been. She nodded and said, "Ssshhh . . . no tell Papa," and then would smile slyly.

February 5, 1917

President Wilson made a speech in support of self-government for Puerto Rico. Now the women on the picket lines are making new signs demanding that he look in his own backyard and give women the right to vote. It seems to me that the farther you are from the White House and the more in need of democracy, the better the chance that Wilson will come to your aid. Kind of odd, if you ask me.

I went into Nell's room to say good night just a few minutes ago and she was pinning up a picture she had gotten of the Women's Ambulance Corps. They were all standing in front of their ambulances somewhere in France in very snappy outfits. They did look good. They wore belted fitted jackets and skirts that buttoned down the front and high boots. I loved their hats. Flat on top with a patent leather bill. And they also wore gloves. I guess it's easier to pick up wounded bodies that are

slippery with blood if you wear gloves. And the ambulances were modern looking — tall boxy vehicles with
doors that fold back and big shiny headlights. It would
be heaven to drive one. Oh, and I forgot, the women
wear ties just like men do!

FEBRUARY 9, 1917

I hate Uncle Bayard. I think he is the most narrow-
minded man I have ever met. Clary has come down with
bronchitis. Father is treating her, and Alma and I and of
course, Mother and Auntie Claire are all to blame. He
found out about Clary going with us to the picket line.
Now he is saying that if it hadn't been for this fool
"woman's thing," as he calls the suffrage movement,
and stupid silly girls (me and Alma) and even sillier
women (Mother and Auntie Claire), his precious Clary,
who does not have "natural sense" — not that we have
any more, he says — would not now be at death's door.
He blames Auntie Claire most of all and his words are
simply poisonous. Father tried to calm him down. He
speaks in such ugly ways. He talked about how poor
Clary's brain is "deficient" and how there is a medical

reason for that. Then he wheeled around and hissed at Auntie Claire and asked what the reason for her brain's weakness was, other than being a woman. Then Father interrupted and told him he couldn't have him talking this way to his wife, especially in front of Alma and me. Uncle Bayard just turned to him and said, "Then I suggest you leave."

Father said, "I shall, but I shall return to treat Clary."

This is a terrible predicament.

FEBRUARY 10, 1917

Clary does not improve. We are all gripped with the worst fears. Alma said a disturbing thing. She said that her mother, who no longer goes to the picket line, said she thought Uncle Bayard almost wished Clary would die, for it would in some way justify his hatred of women's suffrage.

FEBRUARY 11, 1917

Clary still fares poorly but Alma reports that she said an astounding thing in her delirium. "Mama," she said, "I'll be coming with a hot brick for you and Auntie Eleanor — just a minute." I nearly cried when I heard this. Clary's life has always been dull because there are so few things she can do. She doesn't know how to read or write. She cannot really follow games well enough to play. She is rather large and ungainly, and when she tries to dance at parties she looks sort of funny, so her father has always discouraged her from dancing in public. She has had comfort in her life but I think very little real joy or any interesting experiences. Carrying those bricks to the picket line for Clary was a real adventure. We did it for a couple of days after the first time, and the policemen were so nice to her and she learned a few of their names and those of the women.

FEBRUARY 12, 1917

I was kept busy today. Nell sent a note to Miss Pruitt's that as soon as I finished school I should rush to the Woman's Party headquarters because help was needed.

It is all because of Lincoln's birthday, which is today, and the Silent Sentinels have special banners that they are carrying. I had to help finish stitching them up. Mrs. Belmont was there and had a number of her maids with her. Everyone was sewing like crazy. Here is what one said: AFTER THE CIVIL WAR, WOMEN ASKED FOR POLITICAL FREEDOM. THEY WERE TOLD TO WAIT — THIS WAS THE NEGRO'S HOUR.

The old colored lady, Mrs. Belmont's upstairs maid stitching next to me on this banner, just snorted. She said softly, "I ain't noticed no Negro hour. I ain't even noticed a Negro minute." I couldn't help but start giggling and she didn't take offense, thank heaven, but seemed to enjoy that I found this funny.

Another banner I stitched on said LINCOLN STOOD FOR WOMEN'S SUFFRAGE 60 YEARS AGO, MR. PRESIDENT. WHY DO YOU BLOCK THE NATIONAL SUFFRAGE AMENDMENT TODAY? WHY ARE YOU BEHIND LINCOLN?

When we got the banners finished I had to run over with them to the picket lines at the White House. Mother was there and Nell but not Auntie Claire. She is still trying to keep the peace at home.

I really am very fond of Doris Stevens. She has been a friend of Mother's and Father's forever. She always gives me a special wink when I arrive, and today she was standing with Lucy Burns. Miss Burns and Alice Paul have worked together from the time they met in England working for women's rights. They were arrested there several times. Mother calls them "some team!" But they are quite different in appearance and manner. Lucy is tall with fiery red hair and is always laughing and making jokes. She is all movement, while Alice Paul is all stillness and repose.

Lucy called me over and said, "Hey, Kat, wanna hear a valentine verse I made up for the president?"

I went over and Lucy bent her head close to my ear. A fiery red tendril whipped across my face in the breeze.

Roses are red
Violets are pink
President Wilson thinks
Women's rights stink.

"I love it," I shrieked. And Lucy Burns did a little jig on the sidewalk to keep her feet warm. I made her repeat it so I could tell Alma.

February 13, 1917

Clary is better! We are all so happy, so relieved. I am going over today and taking with me piles of colored paper, paper doilies, and ribbons, and we are going to make valentines with Clary in her sick room. Marietta has baked special little Valentine's cakes. It will be so much fun.

Later

It was fun. Clary wasn't very good at the cutting at first, but we helped her and she actually improved. She loved pasting on the lace trim. Auntie Claire had some very pretty cotton lace left over from some project. We were all having a merry time, decorating valentines and writing verses and eating iced cakes, when Uncle Bayard peeked in. Oh, he was very cheerful and smiled broadly. "So happy to see all my little girls doing so well. What a wonderful thing, making valentines."

Auntie Claire smiled a funny kind of half smile. And all I could think was, Is this the only way for this man to be pleased with females? I mean, for him to call Auntie

Claire a little girl! She is his wife. She is the mother of his eight children. And Mother says she knows his business as well as he does. I guess this is so if she was threatening to tell Uncle Everett not to invest in the gold mine.

February 14, 1917

Clary has completely recovered and Auntie Claire was back on the line this afternoon. Alma didn't dare come. She said her father is fuming. He doesn't know what he can do about her mother because she has such a powerful hold over him. Not only with what she knows about the gold mine, but she also has threatened to hire an attorney if she has to get her own money out, money that our grandfather left to both Mother and Auntie Claire. But Alma said there is plenty he could do to her. "Like what?" I asked.

"Send me to Ashmont." Ashmont is the old Minette plantation down in Maryland and Alma hates it. Her father's mother lives there. If she were sent there she might have to have a private tutor. Alma says he's been looking for an excuse to get her out of Miss Pruitt's, which he thinks is too "progressive." If she goes to

Ashmont she will be taught to be "a fine Southern lady," he says.

FEBRUARY 15, 1917

Snowing and sleeting today, but I wouldn't have missed going to the White House this afternoon. The numbers in the picket line have tripled and we hear that around the country other states are having similar demonstrations. But today was special. It was Susan B. Anthony's birthday, so there were more people than ever. Alma and I had actually helped work on a special Susan B. Anthony banner for this day. People, thousands of them, stopped and read the words she had spoken during the Civil War: WE PRESS OUR DEMAND FOR THE BALLOT AT THIS TIME IN NO NARROW, CAPACIOUS, OR SELFISH SPIRIT, BUT FROM PUREST PATRIOTISM FOR THE HIGHEST GOOD OF EVERY CITIZEN, FOR THE SAFETY OF THE REPUBLIC.

FEBRUARY 16, 1917

Tonight I was doing my homework. I was having trouble with a math problem. We had to do a problem two ways — one way using percentages and another way using fractions. I am very good at the fraction way but I really don't understand percentages. I should be getting the same answer either way, but I don't. So I went to Father's study. There was just a little slice of light coming out the door. I heard Mother and Father talking in very low voices. There was a terrible urgency in their tone. I was starting to make out the words and then one word I heard quite distinctly. DIVORCE!

February 19, 1917

I have been beside myself with worry. I cannot believe that Mother and Father would divorce. But maybe Father has had enough of Mother and the Silent Sentinels and the picket line and suffrage. I watch them carefully now for any signs. I think perhaps they are not as affectionate as they used to be, although they were never ones for great displays. But every now and then Father would give Mother's shoulder a squeeze or there would just be a certain look that would pass between them. And here I thought I would wind up being an orphan. But the child of a divorce! They both seem freakish. No one gets divorced. Oh, there was once a girl in Cassie's class at Miss Pruitt's and her parents were divorced. And she lived with her grandmother because her mother had to work.

FEBRUARY 20, 1917

I can't mention my divorce fears to Alma because I think she thinks I whine too much. I had told her about my orphan fears and finally she said I was becoming tiresome. And I can't talk to Nell about it because she is all caught up with the Woman's Party convention that is to happen soon, right around the time of President Wilson's inauguration for his second term, which is to be March 4. They are planning all sorts of demonstrations. I was supposed to go over to the headquarters and help make banners but I made an excuse. I play these strange games with myself. When I was walking home from school today, I thought, *I shall close my eyes and when I stop if I am standing on a sidewalk crack it means Mother and Father are getting divorced. If I am between, it means they won't.* I know it's stupid but I just can't help myself.

February 21, 1917

Miss Pruitt says I am distracted. She's right. But what am I supposed to say? My mother and father might be getting divorced. She made me stay after school for extra help in math from her sister, Miss Janet. Her name is Pruitt too but there can't be two Miss Pruitts in one school, so the second one is Miss Janet. Miss Janet helps with the little ones. She smells funny and she reminds me of a soggy old tea bag. She has about three strands of hair on her whole head and still she wears a hair net. She wears a locket around her neck and the rumor among the girls is that she has in it the picture of her fiancé, who was killed in the Civil War.

Apparently Miss Janet is a whiz with percentages, although it's hard to imagine Miss Janet whizzing at anything. She creeps along at a snail's pace and she brushes every paper three times with the palm of her hand before she begins to write. Then she sticks the nib of her pencil on her tongue, and adjusts her spectacles, pats her three strands of hair, and finally in a very creaky voice begins to explain percentages. But I don't really pay attention. You see, I must sit so close to her that I notice all sorts of other odd things about her. She has a mole with a hair growing out of it on her chin. What a shame. If only that hair could be moved to her scalp. And then her hands are all speckly with purple blotches and her veins stand out maybe a quarter of an inch. Although she is quite thin her feet puff up over the edges of her shoes like balloons. I know this because I dropped my pencil and when I bent over to pick it up I was astonished by her feet. It was as if they belonged on another body.

Needless to say, my knowledge of percentages was not advanced.

FEBRUARY 22, 1917

I ate an apple and threw the core at the trash pail in the kitchen when I got home from school today. I thought, *If it goes in the pail Mother and Father are not getting divorced.* Well, it didn't go in the pail. It didn't go on the floor either. It hit Marietta square in the chest and went right down her dress. She was just walking through! Good Lord, did she squawk. Well, that did it. I started bawling my eyes out.

"What's wrong with you, chile?" She came up and put her arms around me. "What's wrong? What's wrong?" But I couldn't even get the words, or the word out.

Finally I did. "Divorce," I sputtered.

"Who's getting a divorce, chile?"

"Mother and Father," I gulped. And then everything just rushed out, and I mean everything! About being an orphan, my problem with percentages, and how I hated having to work with Miss Janet and the mole with the hair and the feet like balloons. About Nell and the stupid ambulance corps. Finally Marietta blew the air out through her lips so hard that they made that funny vibrating noise — *prrrippp.*

"Honey, it ain't your folks that be gettin' the divorce." She said this with such sureness in her voice that it made me stop my blubbering. She pushed me back a little in her arms and I looked straight into her face.

"Who is it?" I asked.

"If anybody it may be your Auntie Claire. It ain't for sure they be doing it but Juby done overheard and I guess you done overheard your mama and daddy talking, right?" I nodded slowly.

I felt the strangest mixture of sensations. Relief, naturally, but then oddness. It was so odd. And then it hit me. Poor Alma! And here I had been whining to her all the while about being an orphan, and complaining about Nell and the ambulance corps. How will Auntie Claire and Uncle Bayard ever get divorced? What will happen to all those little babies and Clary? I think I have been very selfish to be so concerned with my own fears, but now how can I bring this up with Alma? I mean, I am sure I am not supposed to know and maybe Alma doesn't know. I just don't understand why life has to be so complicated and I certainly can't believe that on the first page of this diary, a mere six weeks ago, I said that my life was so dull I wouldn't have anything to write about. Well, it's not as if my life is tremendously exciting, but I sure do have a lot to write about.

FEBRUARY 23, 1917

Alma and I went to the Ardmore and finally had our banana split. When Alma and I eat a banana split together we do it perfectly. I know that sounds stupid but we just know how to eat one together. No one gets piggy and tries to hog all the sauce. Alma knows that I like to eat the banana part first and then get to the ice cream. So she never invades my ice-cream territory. See, we're just so close we know without speaking how to behave toward each other in the most civilized manner. It is no work being with

Alma. It is only friendship and it is as easy as rowing down a quiet, still river on a summer day. When Alma and I grow up and are real young ladies we are going to make a grand tour of Europe together, if there's anything left after the war. We have already started working on the itinerary.

February 24, 1917

Father has come home in a complete dither from his men's club. We shall read all about it in the paper tomorrow, he says. The British have intercepted a coded message between the Germans and the Mexicans. The Mexicans had offered bases to German submarines on the coast of Mexico — on the shores of our continent! This is too close! It is almost as if I can smell the mustard gas. Nell won't even have to go abroad to join the ambulance corps — just south of the border! It is so scary. Father says the president is hopping mad. The coded message is called the Zimmerman telegram and it will be published in the paper in the next few days. This really is starting to look like war. My worries about orphandom (for lack of a better word) are taking a backseat to being blinded by mustard gas or blown up by a bomb.

FEBRUARY 25, 1917

Father came home with the evening paper. There it was in the headlines in the biggest, blackest letters I've ever seen. MEXICO SWAPS U-BOAT BASES FOR TEXAS IN DEAL WITH GERMANS. BRITISH INTELLIGENCE BREAKS CODE OF ZIMMERMAN TELEGRAM.

Mother and Nell were still on the picket line, but Alma was spending the night. I couldn't believe it but Uncle Bayard let her because she convinced him I needed help with percentages for a math test tomorrow and I will help her with Latin. It was a different evening. We did very little studying but Father seemed happy for the company. He invited us into his study. We discussed the Zimmerman telegram. He says it is unbelievable that the kaiser would presume to offer such a deal to the Mexican government. How could they simply give away a state of ours? I don't understand it. "Well, that means war," Father said very calmly, looking at Alma and me with his steady dark eyes.

My lips moved around the words but no sound came out. I so much wanted to ask a question but I couldn't make my mouth do it. Finally in a small voice I did not even recognize I muttered, "Father, must you go to war?"

He couldn't hear me. Then Alma spoke up very clearly and told him I was worried to death about his going away to war to be a doctor and then with Aunt Eleanor still on the picket line I would be orphaned.

"Kat!" Father exclaimed. Then he rushed to assure me that first of all he is too old to be called up to go to the Great War. He had already been called in the event of war to help train the younger doctors at hospitals in Washington, D.C. and Maryland because of his experience in the Spanish-American War. He convinced me I wouldn't be orphaned but he said my mother will still be on the picket line. And Alma's too. It is a noble cause even though it is an inconvenient one. Father snorted.

There was this long silence that seemed to widen into a huge gulf and I suddenly knew with absolute certainty that we were all thinking about the same thing: Uncle Bayard. His name hung in the air as big and bold as the letters in the headlines. "I wish," Alma said in a soft but steady voice, "my father could be like you, Uncle Alfred."

All the light went out of Father's eyes and he suddenly seemed old and tired. He paused a long time. "I want you to know, Alma, that come what may, you shall always have a place here in this house." I looked first to

Father and then to Alma. They were locked in each other's gaze. I knew in that moment that it was true. Her parents would get divorced. I think Alma is the bravest person I know.

Later

Alma and I talked all night long. She said she had been longing to tell me about the divorce although it is not for sure. I feel so stupid about how I have been all wrapped up in myself, worrying about being an orphan. I honestly think she did not want to tell me because she considers me too immature. And she's right! She says her worst fear is that she and her younger siblings will all be sent to Ashmont, her grandparents' plantation in Maryland. But she says she will run away before that. I told her she only has to run away to here. She says she doesn't think her father will ever let her move in here. We are too "Yankee" for him. It is true that a lot of my family came from Boston, but some people, such as Uncle Bayard, just never have gotten over the Civil War.

February 27, 1917

Everybody is getting quite excited in anticipation of the president's inauguration for his second term. The Woman's Party is planning some sort of big demonstration. Women from all over are coming for a convention right before the inauguration, barely a week away on March 4. Mother is quite busy because I guess they will be doing big things for the inauguration. Mother is on the special board to plan these activities, but not Auntie Claire. Nell said that would be the straw that broke the camel's back, meaning Uncle Bayard would split in two, I suppose, if his wife were on such a board. So I asked her about the divorce. I couldn't believe it — Nell's jaw dropped in utter shock. Nell tends to have a kind of know-it-all look, but now her face was blank and those fierce dark eyes of hers just opened wide. "You don't know?" I was stunned. I have never known anything my older sisters, Cassie and Nell, didn't. It felt terrific! You cannot imagine how awful it is being so much younger. You never get let in on anything. Yes, there are definite problems with being the youngest. But I had promised myself that I would not be so selfish in my thoughts and dwell on my misfortunes. As long as I am not orphaned and there is no divorce in my family I count myself lucky.

February 28, 1917

For our eyes only, diary, I am announcing right now that I plan to be sick tomorrow. Miss Pruitt says one more session with Miss Janet and I should be set with percentages. I say one more session with Miss Janet and I will be either asphyxiated from her mothball-y smell, or bored to death, or have more bad dreams about her mole with the hair.

Father has to go to Maryland very early tomorrow. I can use this ruse only when he is away, because, after all, he is a doctor. But I plan to start it tonight. I shall begin to complain of a headache after dinner. Then I have my own private hot water bottle, and if I time it right and fill it with hot water and put it on my brow for five minutes, I will feel damp and sweaty when Mother comes to kiss me good night. She will then run downstairs to get Father. It will take her at least four minutes to come back with him, and I will have a few more minutes of hot water bottle application. Then Father will come in and touch my head and feel my glands. I actually have a way of swallowing and holding air in the back of my throat that makes them seem a teeny tiny bit swollen. It is an art that Alma and I have developed. Then he will go and get a thermometer. It of course will register normal because I won't have had a chance to work my wonders on it yet. I can do that only when he is away. But Father will furrow his brow and say, "She might be coming down with something." Music to my ears!

In the morning when Father is gone I shall complain bitterly of a headache and scratchy throat. I will not actually say "scratchy." I find it is more effective to say "dry" or "dusty" or sometimes "sandy." Of course more work with the hot water bottle will be needed. I will be absolutely clammy by the time Mother arrives with the thermometer. Now, when Mother sticks the thermometer in my mouth she always says, "Be right back." Then she goes to make phone calls or instruct Marietta. Needless to say by the time she has returned I will have managed to stick the thermometer under scalding hot water in the bathroom so it reads at least 100 degrees. But Mother keeps me home if it is 99. So that is the plan. I shall rest comfortably in bed, avoid Miss Janet, and might even practice my percentages. Anything not to ever see those balloon feet and the hairy mole and be engulfed in the mothball smell.

MARCH 1, 1917

It worked! I'm having a very pleasant day in bed. Mother is off at the picket line, of course. Marietta always comes up with cinnamon toast and tea and Jell-O when I am "sick." I love Jell-O. I think Jell-O is the most fabulous invention ever. I think it is right up there with the automobile. Mr. Jell-O should really be as rich as Henry Ford, in my book. I might do some percentages but I am reading *Ivanhoe*. It is a novel by Sir Walter Scott all about a chivalrous knight who returns to England from the crusades. There are two beautiful heroines in it — Rowena and Rebecca, the Jewess. They are both lovely. I can't decide which one I would most like to be, although I know it is difficult being Jewish, then and now. But Rebecca is so beautiful. She has jet-black hair and high coloring. So unlike me. I have mousey brown hair that is perfectly straight and eyes that are no color, although

Mother persists in calling them "grazel" because she says they are not quite hazel and not exactly gray.

LATER

Talked on the phone to Alma and now, because I missed school, I might not play left wing in field hockey. Today was the first hockey practice. Not really practice because it was too awful to go outside but they went over to the gym in the Ladies' Metro Club, which we are allowed to use for calisthenics and they did a walkabout hockey game to explain to the new girls about the positions and how you play them. Posy Elder, who clomps around like an elephant, played left wing. I am so mad. Left wing requires speed and quick thinking, neither of which Posy has. You also have to be able to keep a picture of the entire field and everyone's position in your head at all times. I am not sure it was worth it, staying home. I love hockey.

MARCH 2, 1917

Squeaked through the math test. Thank heavens. Alma and I went over to National Women's Party headquarters to help with banners for the inauguration. They say women are flocking in from all over.

Mrs. Belmont came right over to us and gave an especially warm hello to Alma. I think maybe Mrs. Belmont knows about Alma's parents.

MARCH 3, 1917

This is astonishing. A negro lady and her daughter are picketing on the lines. I saw her when I went over to deliver some soup for Mother and Auntie Claire. Auntie Claire said, "It's wonderful, but there go any hopes for Southern congressmen supporting us."

No school tomorrow because of the president's inauguration.

LATER

Mother has come home early from the picket line because she plans to rise at four o'clock in the morning to begin to organize for the march. She is in the group that is to go with a delegation to present to the president the resolutions drawn up at the convention that just took place. They all have very high hopes because President Wilson actually said that he "admired their tenacity." They hope with the great show tomorrow, and so many women coming from the western states, that the president will receive their resolutions and take them to Congress. I think there is a very good chance. To think that this picket line has been going on for nearly three months. Oh, how wonderful it would be to have Mother back. I miss her when I come home from school. She always used to be here to open the door for me. And I think it has been more than a week since she has sat down to dinner with us. Yes, I know I am being selfish. Alma would never complain this way, and poor Alma has only her awful father left at home. I at least have a very fine, loving father who tries hard to understand everybody.

MARCH 4, 1917

It was three-thirty in the morning and I heard something
stirring in my room and then I smelled Mother. She always has a powder-fresh scent about her, and she was
bending over to kiss me before she left in the pitch-
blackness of the new day. "Oh, I didn't mean to wake
you. Just wanted to give you a kiss." Mother looked absolutely radiant in the darkness, her brown eyes shining.
She seemed to just tingle with excitement. I was suddenly alert and not at all sleepy.

"Oh, Mother, can I go with you?"

"It's awful out there," she said. I turned to the window and saw sleet and rain slashing across the pane.
The wind drove the rain so hard it was almost falling
sideways.

It was a real gale and my mother, like a stalwart ship,
was sailing out right into the teeth of it and with such
hopes! I watched her through the window as she walked
down the street, lashed by the wind. Two more women
joined her at the corner. They walked past the admiral's
statue. I am so proud of my mother. She is as brave as
any admiral who ever sailed any sea, but Father is right,

it is inconvenient. I pray that President Wilson sees reason. Then all this might soon end.

MARCH 5, 1917

It is late. A terrible gloom has settled over our house and seems to seep out of every crack. I watch Mother. She has sat with her hand on her cup of tea for over twenty minutes and has not taken a sip. She keeps muttering the same words: "The gate where Mrs. Wilson's clothes and other packages are left. That gate — that is where they wanted us to leave the resolutions." Then she squinches her eyes shut tight as if trying to banish the very picture.

You see, what happened was really awful. I even saw much of it with my own eyes, as did Alma. More than a thousand women marched in the procession yesterday morning. Mother, as I said, left at three-thirty in the morning. But Alma and I did not get there until close to nine. There were so many women and so many women's daughters had come to watch that it was not hard to join the procession. It was like a parade, so they didn't have the rules of the picket line about having to be twenty-one. Anyone in America can join a parade. And we did. We even helped carry banners on the poles. The poles were so newly varnished that they became sticky in our hands what with all the rain.

We marched up Pennsylvania Avenue. Mother and Auntie Claire were at the head with the women who were to deliver the resolutions to the president. The streets were lined with spectators huddled under umbrellas. The rain never stopped and the gusty winds took many an umbrella or often turned one inside out. Alma and I were as snug as bugs in rugs, for Father had given both of us old mackintoshes left over from the Spanish-American War. He had liked his first one so much that he had purchased two others. Mother had one tailored to fit her just before the picket lines started. Ours did not fit, especially mine. I looked as if I were standing in a hole. Alma's, because she is taller, fit better. In any case, we were warm and dry.

There were bands for the inauguration and they had already started playing rousing tunes like the "Battle Hymn of the Republic." As we approached the White House we noticed there were hundreds of policemen. The lady next to me said they had brought in police from

Baltimore. "The president must have been scared to death to bring in these coppers."

When we got to the White House gates we were shocked to find them locked. Alma saw an opening in the line to where Auntie Claire and Mother stood by the gates with Lucy Burns, Mrs. Belmont, Alice Paul, and Miss Ann Martin, the leaders of the delegation. Somehow we managed to get very close and heard everything. Miss Martin spoke to the guard very politely. "We have come to present some important resolutions to the president of the United States."

"I have orders to keep the gates locked, ma'am."

"But there must be some mistake. Surely the president does not mean to refuse to see at least . . ."

He cut her off. "Those are my orders, ma'am."

"Will you carry a message to the president that we are waiting to see him?" Miss Martin asked. The guard left for a few minutes and then came back.

"I have orders to answer no questions and to carry no messages." He then directed the delegation to an entrance where they could leave their resolutions, and that was when my mother asked what that entrance was used for.

"Mrs. Wilson's packages — her shopping."

The entire suffrage movement, women's right to vote, had been considered no more important than some department store gewgaw that Mrs. Wilson had purchased on her latest shopping expedition. It was terrible. The women were incensed. But did they stop marching? No. All day through the stinging wind-driven rain they continued, and more and more women joined them. Then late that afternoon the big luxurious limousine carrying the president and his wife rolled out of the White House grounds and through the gates. We were all standing there with our banners. But the president and Mrs. Wilson looked straight ahead as if their heads had been bolted onto their shoulders.

All hopes were dashed in that instant. After three months of picketing nothing has come of it, and my mother, who set out this morning before the break of day so full of hope, looks broken herself now, muttering the same words over and over in the wing chair and not touching her tea.

MARCH 10, 1917

All of us have had the most miserable colds. I missed several days of school but now I look forward to Cassie coming home for a school vacation. The weather is much better. Hockey practice begins next week. I hope that all this nonsense about Posy playing left wing will just disappear. I can't wait to see Cassie. I want to hear about college and her beaus and living in the dormitory at Radcliffe and what Boston is like. Nobody ever talks about anything fun around here. It's all the picket line, women's suffrage, and the Great War. It makes me sound like a very trivial person, doesn't it? Well, perhaps I am. You know, not everybody can be born for great and noble causes. And that's a fact.

MARCH 13, 1917

Cassie has come home and all she wants to talk about is great and noble causes. Yes, she wants to quit college and join the picket line and then Nell started talking to her about the Women's Ambulance Corps. And I wanted to hear about boyfriends and at least Boston and the swan boats. Yes, they have these boats that you can sit on that are shaped like huge swans and they paddle you around in them on the pond in the Boston Public Gardens. Mother and Father will not let her quit college, however. They are very much in agreement on this.

All right, I know that what I am going to say next would cause Mother and all the women in the National Woman's Party to have conniptions. But Cassie is so beautiful that I think it is a shame that she does not currently have a beau and is no longer interested in going to parties and tea dances. When she came home after her freshman year that is all she talked about and we went to the department store and got her some lovely tea-dancing dresses. Cassie's hair is as curly as mine is straight and it has wonderful auburn highlights. I think it is a complete waste that all she wants to do is join the picket line and that all she talks about is how none of the boys she knows at Harvard believes in women having the vote. Therefore she will have nothing to do with them. When I tried to reason with her she blurted out, "You want me to end up with another Uncle Bayard?" Of course not, but there must be something in between. She and Nell just sigh wearily over what I guess they consider my ignorance.

March 15, 1917

Young Bayard, or Barney as everyone calls Alma's brother, came over to take Cassie to a country club dance out in Silver Spring. She very reluctantly had agreed to go before she came home. She looked lovely in an old printed silk voile dress of Mother's embroidered with pearls and bugle beads. Of course Cassie would look fabulous in a laundry bag.

Later

Holy smokes! Cassie came back early from the dance tonight. She was delivered to our door by an absolutely incensed Barney, who said that she had made a spectacle of herself. Cassie fumed at him. "That crowd needs a few more spectacles — no pun intended, but in terms of vision they are absolutely myopic and in terms of social conscience they are Neanderthals."

"You don't shout down the attorney general of the United States, Cassandra," Barney hissed.

"What?" My father stood gasping in his smoking

jacket. I had come down in my robe, and Mother and Nell just stood on the stairs looking confused.

Here is what happened. They were at the country club and Cassie said they were at a table with a group of young people and having a very nice time. A gentleman named Mr. Gregory, the attorney general of the United States, came over to the table to say hello to a niece. He commented on how nice it was to see young women all in silk and dancing and having such a good time and that he was happy that none of them was mixed up with the suffragists who nearly spoiled the inauguration. Cassie says she didn't say a thing until he said, "You know what I would do if I was one of those policemen? I'd just take a hose out with me and when the women came out with their banners, why, I'd squirt the hose on them." There was a lot of tittering around the table. Then he said, "If you can make what a woman does look ridiculous you can sure kill it."

That was too much for Cassie. She jumped up and said, "Mr. Gregory, my mother and aunt were among those women. What right would these policemen have to attack these women? Did it ever occur to you as the highest officer of the law of the land that squirting water from a hose on law-abiding citizens might make you and the office of the attorney general, not to mention the government, look ridiculous? I think you should resign."

Well, Mother sank down on the step where she stood and Nell let out a whoop and Father just looked plain amazed. I have to admit I am really proud of Cassie. Imagine calling down the attorney general of the United States of America. I suppose it is more exciting than riding on a swan boat. But Father and Mother are still making her go back to school for the term.

MARCH 16, 1917

Idiot cousin Barney blabbed to his father about what happened at the country club. Uncle Bayard called up Father and ranted on about Cassie's behavior and how it was going to be the ruination of him and his family and that they would all get thrown out of the country club. And now he forbids any contact between the children of his household and ours! Father looked quite gray when he hung up the phone. He muttered something I didn't understand, which was "to forbid is to invite trouble." I don't know how I am to avoid contact with Alma. We go to the same school.

March 19, 1917

Worst day of my life. Unbelievable that all this could happen on one day. I guess I should list these in order of worldwide importance, which has very little to do with my feelings. (1) The Germans sank three American merchant ships in the last two days so we are going to enter the war. (2) Tsar Nicholas was overthrown in Russia. No more Romanovs after three hundred years of their ruling and people are killing each other in the streets of Moscow. (3) Alma is being sent to Ashmont!

It is very odd to contemplate these three separate things or events. They all are disconnected, but in some way I feel that they might be connected, in ways we cannot see. I feel that we are on the brink of a changing world and maybe it begins or ends in little households like ours and Alma's. I cannot bear the thought of Alma being at Ashmont.

MARCH 20, 1917

She's gone already. Just whisked away. No time for good-byes. All of her schoolbooks and notebooks left in her desk. I could not believe it when Miss Pruitt said Alma Minette had been withdrawn. I never expected it to happen so soon. I couldn't stand it. Still can't. I'm going to do *something.* I'm not sure what. When I found out this morning, I simply could not bear to be in school another minute. I pretended I was sick and asked to go home. So here I am. Marietta, my usual source of information, is out marketing.

LATER

I decided to find out myself what's going on, so I went over to Alma's house. The more I walked the madder I got, until I arrived at Alma's and knocked on the door as loud as I could. Juby came to answer. I could see she had been crying. "What's going on?" I asked.

"Nothing no good," she answered. Then Henry came. Haughty, arrogant — gosh, I hate him. So Henry said he'd handle this.

I demanded to know where Alma was.

"Gone to Ashmont with Clary and the young ones," Henry said.

"Without saying good-bye?"

"No good-byes were needed," he replied stiffly.

What a pathetic response. When he turned to go inside, for we had been standing on the front stoop, I kicked him right in the seat of his pants. He went sprawling. I really didn't know my legs were that strong. I mean, I should be playing soccer instead of hockey. By the way, I am going to be left wing. But it seems to mean very little now in the scope of things.

March 21, 1917

I am being punished for kicking Henry in the pants. It's no punishment, really. I just have to come home directly from school every afternoon for two weeks. It would be too sad to go to the Ardmore without Alma. To eat a banana split alone is unthinkable, and even though lime rickey season is right around the corner, it just wouldn't be the same sitting there all by myself sucking that fizzy greenness through a straw. You know, Alma never slurped or made sucking noises with her straw. I do. I couldn't stand listening to my own disgusting slurping without Alma's chatter to camouflage it.

The real problem is no one will tell me anything about Alma's "vanishing," as I now think of it. I asked Mother and all she said was, "It's not only Alma, dear. It's Clary and Beauregard and Gerald and Halsey and Davis. Auntie Claire is beside herself."

"Are you going to do anything about it?" I asked.

"I really can't do much. It's a matter for lawyers, really. It's all very complicated."

I decided to have a visit with Marietta the first chance I got.

P.S. A special session of Congress was called. It's all about whether we should go to war.

MARCH 22, 1917

Went up to Marietta's room on the fourth floor late last night. She claims I scared the daylights out of her, tapping on the door. "Thought you were some dang German!" This irritated me. All anybody can think about is the war. I want to think about Alma. I had forgotten how teeny tiny Marietta's room is. It is one-quarter the size of mine. She, of course, keeps it four times as neat as I do. I just came out point-blank and asked her about Alma.

"He done kidnapped dem children. Evil. No good evil."

This is what I needed to hear. No mincing words. No talk of lawyers. "How did he do it?"

"He done got Joss to stuff 'em all in that Packard and drove 'em down to Ashmont in the middle of the night."

"But what about Auntie Claire?"

"Well, what do you suppose? She started screamin' her head off when she found out. It seems Mr. Minette put some powder in her tea that night when she come home from the picket line so she slept real sound. She didn't find out until late in the morning when she finally woke up."

Powder in the tea! I was stunned. This was criminal.

"Yep. Juby saw him do it."

I didn't know how she could stand living in that house a minute longer.

But she had gone over to Mrs. Belmont's, Marietta told me.

"Why didn't she come here?" I asked.

"Oh, she probably don't want to drag your mama and daddy into it and I tell you, Mr. Minette, he be scared of Mrs. Belmont. She's one powerful lady."

Told you, diary, when you want to find out something you go to Marietta. No beating around the bush with her. I am not any happier. I mean, Alma is still gone, but at least I know the whole story. I cannot stand adults who do not give children complete information. I shall never do that as a parent. Never never never.

MARCH 23, 1917

Exactly two weeks until my fourteenth birthday and Alma's. We always had a joint celebration.

MARCH 25, 1917

A letter from Alma! My hands are still trembling. I have read it ten times and they still tremble. It was just as Marietta described. Alma is devastated. She is most worried about her mother and the effect all this will have on her. She says the babies, Halsey and Davis, whine all day. Beauregard is better because they have given him a pony. She says her grandma, Sunday Minette (real Southerners often have strange names), is unbearable. Here is exactly what she writes about her:

"Granny Sunday is the most ill-named woman in the world. She is like a perpetual dark cloud looming on the horizon. She squawks at all of us constantly but gets a particular edge in her voice when she speaks to me. You see, I remind her of that 'Yankee woman' — that's how she still refers to Mother — who married her precious son. She blames all of Clary's problems on that 'thin Yankee blood from up North.' She is going to try to turn me into a proper Southern girl, so she insists that I read less. I told her flat out that I thought first of all this was an insult to Southern women and that I had no intention of reading less."

I say, Bravo for Alma. Alma is so incredibly smart. She thinks of clever things to say and does not act impulsively like me and go around kicking stupid men in the pants — although I am still glad I did it. I am going to write her right away.

March 29, 1917

It was a real lime rickey kind of day. Hot and sunshiny.
The cherry blossoms all bursting out. There is something
odd about it all, however — our first real spring day and
all anyone talks about is war. I hear about what is happening over there on the front, as they call it. I see the
terrible reports in the newspapers and the pictures of
wounded, the fire and smoke from bombs. And here
in Washington there are pink cherry blossoms bursting in
the air. What an odd world we live in.

April 2, 1917

What a strange evening. Went with Father to see the
president's motorcade drive up to Capitol Hill. We stood
in a soft drizzling rain with thousands of people as we all
watched the president escorted by a troop of cavalry go
to Congress to ask for war. The Capitol, white and misty
in the evening light, glowed like a huge dim pearl. The
crowds were unusually silent. Mother stood with a con-
tingent from the National Woman's Party. There were
new signs: EVERYONE'S LIBERTY IS SACRED. DO NOT FORGET

WOMEN'S SUFFRAGE. Another read FREEDOM ABROAD AND AT HOME AS WELL.

Father shook his head. "They shouldn't be pushing now." I knew what he meant. He felt that the women should step aside in this somber moment, that it would harm their cause more than help it. Nell was not standing with Alice Paul and Mother and Auntie Claire and Mrs. Belmont. I saw her with another group. I knew that the division within the Women's Party concerning the war was becoming sharper. There were many like Nell who did want the United States to enter the war. I am not sure how I feel.

April 3, 1917

Read President Wilson's war message that he delivered to Congress last night in this morning's paper. It was very stirring. He wants to make "the world safe for democracy." These are his very words. I copy them from the paper exactly. "We are at the beginning of an age in which it will be insisted that the same standards of conduct and of responsibility for wrong done shall be observed." Can't he see that it is not only Germany that has done wrong, but also that here at home there is a wrong because women can't vote? It is as if there are two sets of rules — one for Europe and one for here.

APRIL 4, 1917

The war resolution passed in the Senate today. Eighty-two senators for it, six against it.

Nell and Mother give each other icy looks. Mother seems to excuse Father more than Nell about his views on entering the war. Auntie Claire came for dinner. Now everyone speaks of her divorce very casually. It is nothing, I guess, next to war. Mrs. Belmont is helping her get a good lawyer. She might be giving her money, although I think Auntie Claire has a lot of her own because Mother does. They are sisters, after all, and my grandfather would have treated them equally.

April 6, 1917

Today I turned fourteen and America went to war. It's Good Friday. (Hah!)

April 8, 1917

My official birthday celebration was this evening. It was arranged around the war and mother's picketing schedule and Father's schedule at the hospital and an appointment Auntie Claire had with a lawyer. I was squeezed in, so to speak. I don't mean to sound ungrateful, but in truth, despite the nice presents, my birthday seemed a big inconvenience to everyone except myself. Auntie Claire was pretty glum. How could she help but think of Alma, for it's her birthday as well? Marietta did make all my favorite foods. Beans with redeye gravy, mashed potatoes, fried chicken, and NOTHING green. I hate green food — except for lime rickeys, that is. She made a lovely cake. Nothing disgusting in it like nuts or raisins. Just a nice yellow cake all slathered with white frosting. I love frosting. I could tell Auntie Claire was fighting back tears when they brought in the cake all lit up and started singing "Happy Birthday." I mean, for fourteen years it's been "Happy Birthday, Alma and Kat" (alphabetical order).

I sent Alma a whole box of stuff. Mother gave me the money and Marietta took me shopping. The best present was the book *Pride and Prejudice* by Jane Austen. I had just finished reading it myself. It's a wonderful story and Elizabeth Bennet, the main character, is massively intelligent and lovely in spite of having a very silly mother. And then there is this arrogant young man — well, I can't give it all away. Anyhow I loved it and went to Frobishers' bookstore and bought the same copy I have — pale blue binding with gold fleur-de-lis stamped on the cover. I also bought Alma a whole packet of wonderful-smelling sachets and a fashion magazine.

April 10, 1917

They speak of sending an expeditionary force of close to a hundred thousand young men to France. And today I saw pictures in the paper that were really terrifying. Dead bodies, their limbs at odd angles strewn in a trench and above them, men in swirling smoke. There was another picture of a merchant ship in sheets of flames after a German U-boat had struck it with torpedoes, and then another of a soldier carrying a wounded man whose face was covered with blood.

Mother is on her way to the picket line. They will carry signs that fling President Wilson's words back to him: WE SHALL FIGHT FOR THE THINGS WE HAVE ALWAYS HELD NEAREST TO OUR HEARTS . . . FOR DEMOCRACY and so on. I am not sure how I feel about Mother going out with these signs when I see such pictures as I have seen in the newspapers. Are the rights of women this important? I mean, men are dying and soon American men will die. I would even feel sorry for Henry if indeed he had blood pouring from his face as that young fellow in the newspaper.

April 13, 1917

First real hockey practice today. We were supposed to get new uniforms, something more modern, but with the anticipated war shortages we are playing in our same old disgusting maroon tunics with bloomers underneath. I am playing left wing, thank heavens. Deborah Paine is right wing, and Harriet Wilhelm is center. No doubt about it, she has a very unfortunate last name. Coupled with the fact that she is a very aggressive player it was no time before someone started calling her Kaiser Wilhelm, the awful German king who started this whole awful war. Harriet left the field in tears. Miss Hornsby, our gym teacher and hockey coach, blew so hard on her whistle that her eyes bugged out. She is slightly buggy-eyed anyhow. She called an immediate halt to the game. The next thing we knew, Miss Pruitt came marching onto the field and we were all required to stay two hours after school! The entire team. All except of course Harriet Wilhelm. And this is Friday! Friday the thirteenth, I might add.

APRIL 15, 1917

The entire hockey team was made to write a letter to Harriet apologizing for our behavior. Some of us felt so bad that we invited Harriet to go with us to the Ardmore, and we chipped in and bought her an ice-cream soda. Just when we thought everything was going so well Posy Elder said, "Tell me, Harriet, has your family ever considered changing their name?"

Harriet's eyes widened and she appeared stunned. "Why would we ever do that?" she asked.

"Well, you know, because of the unfortunate connection with the kaiser in Germany — such a brute. You wouldn't want people to think you were related."

"Posy!" I gasped. This was simply unbelievable.

But Harriet was equal to the challenge. "That he is a tyrant has nothing to do with me or my family. My mother stands in the picket line alongside Kat's mother and Nancy Abbot's mother. My father is a doctor in the same hospital with Kat's father. He fought in the Spanish-American War and my grandfather fought in the Civil War. We would never think of changing our name."

Posy flushed a furious red. She looked rather Christmasy sucking on a lime rickey and did not say another word for the rest of the time. Some people have no brains.

April 16, 1917

Received a letter and birthday package from Alma today. What a funny coincidence. She sent me a Jane Austen book, *Sense and Sensibility,* along with a beautiful scarf. Nothing improves at Ashmont. If anything it gets worse. Granny Sunday's loathsome sister has arrived — Great-Aunt Dolly. Alma says she looks like a painted doll and her eyes even work like those weighted dolls' eyes so that when you tip the doll one way the eyes roll back and shut, when you tip the other way they open. Sunday and Dolly squabble all day long and Dolly tries to get Alma to be on her side. Dolly's fiancé was killed in the Civil War and she has never married and has worn black ever since. She has a digestive disorder that causes her to belch loudly but because Granny Sunday is slightly deaf she is always saying, "What'd you say, Doll?" And Dolly doesn't like to admit she's belched so she just makes up something. The only good news is that Clary seems to be adjusting. She can go outside more down on the plantation. It is safer and there is a large yard and garden where she spends endless hours and seems quite content. But poor Alma is bored stiff. They say they are going to hire a tutor, but so far no one has been hired. She asked about hockey. She used to play left inner, a very important position. She says Uncle Bayard has come to visit only once and spent the whole time talking with Grandma Sunday — about money,

Alma thinks. She has reason to suspect that he is in very bad shape money-wise.

April 24, 1917

I know for sure Nell is up to something. I am not sure what. I came across her talking in a hushed voice on the upstairs phone and she gave me an absolutely poisonous look. I know that in the National Woman's Party a real line is being drawn between those who favor the war and those who do not.

April 28, 1917

We won our first hockey game! It was against the Madeira School. They are very tough and they have a center that makes Harriet Wilhelm look like a pussycat. These Madeira girls are all huge. All ferocious but actually our team is quicker, more nimble, and we play with our heads as Miss Hornsby keeps screaming at us to do. She actually said one day when our line was advancing down the field and we had left a flank open where the other team could get in, "Play with your brains, you numskulls!" No one took it personally. I actually thought it was very funny.

May 3, 1917

Father came home quite excited this evening. General John Pershing has been appointed head of the American Expeditionary Force. Father knows him, not well, but he served in the Spanish-American War and fought at Santiago. Father had to treat him at a hospital in Key West, Florida, where they brought a lot of the wounded from that war.

"You mean he got wounded?" I asked.

Father hesitated "Er, no. It was more an illness he picked up in the field."

"What?" I asked.

Father blushed slightly. "Dysentery."

"You mean diarrhea?"

"Yes, dear. Very bad water down there."

Not the kind of noble, debilitating war wound one expects from a military hero who is about to command the largest expeditionary force in American history.

MAY 4, 1917

They might pass a Selective Service Act, which will make it possible for the government to call up young men and draft them for the expeditionary force. Millions are needed. Mother and Alice Paul and Lucy Burns are furious.

MAY 6, 1917

This is awful. Whenever I see a picture of General Pershing in the newspaper all I can think of is the embarrassing illness that Father treated him for. I really do have a very small and dull mind, don't I?

MAY 7, 1917

Mother came home today so happy! She says that there is real hope for Auntie Claire getting all her children back. Oh, Lordy! If Alma could come home how happy I would be.

I wanted to write her tonight and tell her but Mother

said not to because she thinks the dreadful Granny Sunday might be reading Alma's mail and the last thing we want to do is tip off the Minettes about what actually might be happening. Uncle Everett is coming to town in a few days to discuss things with the lawyer. It sounds as if Auntie Claire might have to buy back her children. Seems that Alma was right about the money problems.

MAY 10, 1917

The dreadful Great-Aunt Dolly is dead! And Alma found her. Alma wrote me the most wonderful and extraordinary letter about it. I think Alma should be a writer. She really has a gift. I am paraphrasing it here but Alma describes going out onto a veranda where Great-Aunt Dolly had been taking tea. Great-Aunt Dolly was sitting in a rocking chair and her head was back and her eyes were open and rolled up. Of course, you don't expect anyone to be dead, even with their eyes rolled up, I guess — and Alma thought they were like the doll's eyes anyway, so she just came up and gave the chair a little rock to tip them back the other way. Then she noticed that Dolly had this very angry, mad look on her face, "as if,"

Alma wrote, "she had been cheated out of something and just found out." Alma did tip the chair but the eyes did not roll back into place. There were crumbs on the front of her dress and a crochet needle had slid off onto the floor. In that instant Alma knew Great-Aunt Dolly was dead. Granny Sunday pitched a fit, Alma said. You would have thought they loved each other dearly and never fought. The fit lasted about two hours. Then she quickly sent Alma to town to fetch her lawyer. The phone wasn't working or something. So Alma went. She says all Granny Sunday cares about is who Dolly left her money to.

May 12, 1917

Harriet Wilhelm and I are getting to be fairly good friends. We have twice gone to the Ardmore for lime rickeys. She wanted to share a banana split with me today, but quite honestly I don't have the heart. I think that is something I shall do only with Alma. It just seems disloyal to do otherwise.

MAY 13, 1917

Harriet told me something interesting. She has an older sister who has become a friend of Nell's on the picket line. She said that her sister is for the war just like Nell, and that her mother is against it. Furthermore, she heard her sister talking to Nell the other night on the phone in a low voice, and she too felt her sister Margaret was up to something.

MAY 15, 1917

We won another hockey game. So far we have won two and lost two. We are playing much more aggressively than ever before. I wonder if it doesn't have something to do with the war, or maybe for that matter the picket line. There are at least three or four mothers from school on the picket line now. Maybe we just want to prove how tough and ferocious we girls can be. I am not sure, but we all seem to have this new spirit running through us. Two gentlemen the other day stopped and watched through the fence grating of the park where we play. I was on the bench near the fence, so I could see and hear them talking. They watched transfixed as Harriet led the way down the field. Her long legs stretched out and she bellowed commands to the flanking inners. She was sleek and fast and powerful. I heard one of the gentlemen say, "So that's what we have to look forward to if all this suffrage nonsense comes to be. God save us, George." I wanted to turn around and say, "You bet!"

Later

I keep thinking about those two men watching us play hockey, and then I think about how a few weeks ago, when we got in the war I was wondering if Mother should still be picketing. I wondered if women's suffrage was really worth it. I think maybe it is. I mean, those men standing there at the fence were not looking at us as human beings, but as some sort of inferior thing called "female." If we could just realize we are *all* humans and should have all the rights due to human beings. If women's suffrage can help people see people as people, human beings, well, that is worth an awful lot. I really think Sojourner Truth said all this best. I am going to read her speech again before I go to sleep.

May 19, 1917

The Selective Service Act was passed. Now many young men will be called up to go to Europe and fight as part of what they are calling the First Division.

Father goes almost every day to a hospital in Virginia to help with the training of medics and nurses from the American Red Cross. He is gone several evenings a week. It seems that Nell is out nearly every night. And Mother is substituting for Mrs. Stevens on the early evening picket shift, so I eat dinner in the kitchen with Marietta. It's hard to believe that in another couple of weeks the picket line will have been going for six months!

Later

Mother came home really angry with President Wilson — as if this is new. The National Woman's Party is now pressing for a women's suffrage committee in Congress, but the president keeps delaying because he says he can attend only to business that has to do with war. But today a Senate committee passed authorization for an expenditure of ten thousand dollars to build a monument to a dead president! She didn't say which one. She just kept muttering, Imagine ten thousand dollars for a statue of a dead man and nothing for millions of living women. I said she should write it on a banner. She paused a second. Then this funny little smile came across her face and she rushed over and hugged me. "Thank God, Kat, you have a sense of humor. Someone needs one these days." I didn't think I was being funny at all. I was serious.

MAY 29, 1917

Every day it seems that new measures are being passed. They call them "war measures," such as the ones that did not permit us to get new hockey uniforms so as to conserve cloth for the war. Now there are food conservation measures and a war tax bill.

Eleven thousand men so far have been sent to Europe to fight as part of the First Division.

May 30, 1917

Mother and Nell had a terrible fight tonight. Mother was defending Alice Paul, who is a Quaker, and the decision of the Woman's Party, which says that those members who want to engage in the war effort must do so as individuals, not party members. Nell was absolutely screaming and Mother, well, Mother does not scream, but there is never any doubt she is angry. I hate this. I HATE HATE HATE it. All right, I'll say it right now: I might as well be a flowerpot in this household. Nobody pays any attention to me. They all go about business that they think is much more important, and maybe it is, but it is simply not fair. I am fourteen years old. I deserve more attention. Nell and Cassie got their fair share when they were fourteen. There was no darned war going on and no picket line. My very own birthday celebration had to be squeezed in between everyone's noble doings. I am too young to be part of anything and too old to enjoy the benefits of being a cute, chubby little baby who just screams "waaa" and gets her own way.

LATER

I went up to Marietta's. I told Marietta exactly how I was feeling. And Marietta just stared at me like I was the dumbest thing in the world. "Why girl, why don't you just go tell them?"

"Go tell who?"

"Your folks."

"Mother? Father?"

"Those be the only folks you got, far as I know."

She was right. It was so simple.

JUNE 1, 1917

I got up very early this morning and went to Father just like Marietta told me. First of all he was shocked to see me up so early. Father rises at five o'clock. So I told him. I thought it might be hard and I was awfully afraid I might cry. But I didn't. As a matter of fact I felt my voice grow stronger. I broke only once when I said I have no one — even Alma is gone. Father was very still and looked at me with great concentration. Father's eyelids slightly hood his eyes like little triangles. I often joke with him that he has "tepee" eyes — you know, like Indian tepees. But they frame the light in his eyes and that light was like an intense beam focused on me. "Get your wrap," Father said.

"Why? Where are we going?"

"You can come to the hospital with me."

"What about school?"

"What about it? There's less than a week left."

LATER

What a wonderful day. I watched Father teach and do demonstrations and he let me go with him into certain wards. And guess what? I finally understand percentages. Yes, percentages are very necessary in the medical profession. There are beakers that must be filled with 20 percent saline solutions and when Father drew blood or took urine samples he explained to me how they test for certain percentages of this and that. I mean, I could finally work the percentage problems in school, but it was as if I were doing it by rote, just mechanically, and couldn't really understand it. It is so funny when you hook up things to real life how much clearer they become.

Father promises to take me with him at least once a week.

June 4, 1917

Harriet told me that her sister Margaret and Nell, she knows for a fact, have been attending some sort of meetings together and they are not National Women's Party meetings. She thinks it is something to do with the war.

"Are they secret meetings?" I asked.

"I don't know. Are you thinking they are spies, Kat?"

Spies! I nearly died. The thought had never crossed my mind. "No, for heaven's sakes."

"Me neither," said Harriet.

We just think they are afraid to tell anyone they are for the war and that is why they are sneaking around. But one thing we did decide to do is follow them to their next meeting. It should be tomorrow, Harriet says, since she thinks they meet on Tuesdays.

JUNE 5, 1917

Nell is gone! Harriet and I didn't even get a chance to follow her and Margaret to a meeting. They are both gone. They left notes. The meetings they were going to were for the American Fund for the French Wounded, which provides emergency relief for the soldiers in France. They explained that they had been helping to pack boxes of surgical dressings and hospital supplies, and something called "comfort bags," which had clothing and pencils and paper. Then volunteers were recruited through the fund for the Women's Ambulance Corps — the British one. And Margaret and Nell signed up. They are to be stationed somewhere in France. They went to Baltimore last night and shipped out on the *S.S. Fillmore*. Mother is beside herself. She is convinced that a German U-boat will get them mid-Atlantic. Father just holds Mother's hand and says, "There, there, Eleanor."

It is so queer. Less than a week ago Mother and Nell were arguing furiously about whether America should be in this war and now all it comes down to is that Mother does not want her daughter to be in it. I am not saying that she has abandoned her principles. But the reason she does not want Nell to go is not because of her principles. Mother is really scared. I can see it in her eyes. I have never ever seen Mother so frightened before. It is almost as if I can see a flickering light of terror in her eyes and when I see it, it makes something in me cave in a bit. It is not natural to see your own parents frightened. I know Father is scared too but he is more practiced in hiding it. A veil comes down over the tepee eyes. He must have to do this all the time with patients.

JUNE 6, 1917

Cassie came home from college for the summer. She is very mopey but she knows better than to say anything to Mother or Father about dropping out of school for whatever reason or whatever cause. She is very envious of Nell, I can see that. Harriet has told us that a distant cousin of hers taught Nell and Margaret something about driving and that before they left they had learned how to change tires and do something with spark plugs. That seems utterly amazing to me. Father has invited Cassie to join us when he takes me to the hospital. I guess it is all right but I preferred when it was just me.

Tomorrow Father is going with Auntie Claire and Uncle Everett to Ashmont to visit the children. I pray that they come back with Alma. Mother thinks there is a very good chance, because Uncle Bayard's lawyer has up and quit and very few lawyers want to take on the case. Although many people are not for women's rights, no one looks kindly on men who whisk a woman's children away in the middle of the night.

JUNE 8, 1917

I cannot believe what I have to write on this page — the words I must set down. It is three o'clock in the morning and I was awakened by a great commotion downstairs and the sound of a woman crying. Cassie and I were out of our beds in no time. I didn't even put on a wrapper but from the top of the stairs I saw Auntie Claire collapsed in Mother's arms, crying. Clary stood there, mute and trembling and then the little boys — Halsey, Davis, Gerald, and Beauregard — screaming, crying, and whooping around, each in a different state of emotional stress. But no Alma. And then it all spluttered out. Alma has run off. She too has gone to the Great War. She has joined the American Red Cross. She cannot be a real nurse but she is going to work as a volunteer in an army hospital in England. She lied about her age. The worst is that for some reason, Granny Sunday didn't tell Uncle Bayard for two days. Then Uncle Bayard was too scared to tell anyone else and tried to hunt her down himself. But I simply cannot believe it. I cannot believe that Alma has talked her way into the Red Cross, is now crossing an ocean and about to be part of a war. Alma, who is the exact same age as me! I wonder if she thought of me once before she left. I wonder what she is doing this very minute. I wonder if she misses anybody — me, especially. I can't help but wonder.

JUNE 9, 1917

This place is crawling with babies. Halsey came in this morning and started jumping on my bed. Then I heard Marietta on the telephone with Juby telling her to "git on over" and help take care of these "crazy babies." Auntie

Claire seems to have recovered enough to enjoy what children she has left. She is constantly kissing Clary and telling her that they shall be back home in their house on Sixteenth Street in "two shakes." Well, maybe three, Uncle Everett said. He and Father are off to have a meeting with Uncle Bayard.

JUNE 10, 1917

Harriet and I took Clary to the Ardmore for a lime rickey. Then we walked by the picket line. Clary was excited when she spotted Mother and Auntie Claire with their banners. But I was shocked. The two women just behind them were carrying a banner that said, KAISER WILSON PREACHES DEMOCRACY ABROAD AND THWARTS IT HERE. I saw Harriet's brow furrow. There was something terribly shocking about this. We could not help but remember when the girls called Harriet Kaiser Wilhelm. There is something cheap about it — yes, a cheap shot, Father would say. But Clary was so excited. There were other signs, too, demanding that the president do something for democracy at home. We were not the only ones who found it shocking. There were a couple of hecklers in the crowd who were shouting the women down. Loudly! This has never happened before. Most people in the past months would just come and gawk. But these hecklers were yelling insults. "Worse than Germans." The man next to me shouted that just as Mother and Auntie Claire walked by. Then another. "Monster women!" The words exploded behind me. The crowd was getting more agitated. Clary didn't understand. Harriet and I looked at each other and without speaking knew we must leave and get Clary out.

June 11, 1917

Auntie Claire and all of the children are back in their house on Sixteenth Street. Uncle Bayard is living at his men's club. I do feel very sorry for Clary, though. She just does not quite understand what is happening. She does not do well with too many changes. She is back in her old house but Alma and her father are both gone. She is finding it confusing. Mother has asked that I try to spend a little time with her. I do, but it's really boring. How often can you go to the Ardmore for lime rickeys? And I just do not have that much to talk to Clary about.

JUNE 15, 1917

I had a brilliant idea. When I was visiting the hospital with Father in Virginia where he was giving a lecture to Red Cross nurses on hygiene, I heard one of the nurses talking about something she called a victory garden. I asked her what it was and she said it was a garden to grow one's own food to help save supplies for the soldiers overseas. We don't have much of a yard in Washington, but there is one strip that faces south and Mother always puts in flowers. I think we should grow vegetables. I might even consider eating green things if we did this. I told Father about the idea and he thinks it's "A-number-one." That is Father's favorite expression for something that is really good. So on the way back from the hospital we stopped and bought some seeds and he got me a shovel and trowel. We even went by a farm where he had treated the farmer and got some horse manure in a bag. Father says horse manure is very good fertilizer. Tomorrow is Saturday and Father says he will work with me all day on the garden.

P.S. Nearly forgot to tell about Cassie. She went and got herself a job as a streetcar conductor! There is a shortage of conductors because so many here in Washington were young men who have had to join the army. She's on the Ninth Street line that goes right by the Patent Office, and then on to F Street. Mother did not seem that upset. I guess she would rather have a daughter riding the district streetcar line than careening around France in an ambulance. Cassie gets to wear a conductor's uniform with a shiny billed hat and carries a money changer on her belt. The uniform cannot compare to the Women's Ambulance Corps. Nell did promise to write. I hope she sends us a picture.

JUNE 16, 1917

Today was one of the best days of my life. Father and I were out in the yard by seven o'clock in the morning. It took us all morning even with Marietta's and Joss's help to turn the soil. We had to dig in the manure and then

Joss went and got some old newspapers that he tore up
for us and we dug that in too. He said the torn-up newspaper helps keep moisture in the soil. I wore my hockey
tunic and bloomers to work in. They were just right for
this job. When we got all the soil turned Father sug-
gested that Joss go and bring back Clary, that she might
enjoy it. Father really does think of everything. I then
called up Harriet. We all worked together for the rest of
the day. Marietta made us cheese sandwiches and
lemonade, which we ate outside. After lunch we were
ready to plant. We had to give Clary a lot of instructions
at the start but soon she caught on and was able to plant
a straight row of seeds. We planted sweet peas, two
kinds of lettuce, cucumbers, cabbage, tomatoes (we
cheated a bit there, for the farmer who gave us the manure gave us some tomato plants), carrots, and potatoes.
Marietta showed us how you cut the eyes out of old
potatoes and put them in the ground to make new ones
grow. Very clever arrangement, I think, or as Grandma
Bowen used to say, "God works in mysterious ways."
Who would ever have thought those old potato eyes
could sprout new life? Oh, we also planted radishes,
which I loved. I like red things.

Father whistled the whole time we worked. I rarely

hear Father whistle but he did. It was that new catchy tune written about joining the war, by the songwriter George M. Cohan. And Harriet knew all the words. It goes, "Over there, over there, send the word . . . the yanks are coming."

Late in the afternoon Mother and Cassie arrived home and came out to see what we were doing. I thought maybe Mother would be upset but she seemed very pleased. I said, "So you don't mind?"

And she said, "Why should I mind, dear girl?"

"I thought maybe because of the war and how you feel about Nell and Alma."

Her eyes almost filled and she said, "You are doing a good thing and look how happy you all are." She looked at Father and Clary in particular. "The whole point, dear, is for everyone, no matter what their sex, to be able to participate fully in life. I cannot think of a better way than putting things into the soil to grow. This strip of land was never anything but a scratchy patch. Now look at what you've turned it into — this rich, dark earth and the rows so neatly planted." She turned to Clary and said, "My, what a fine job you've done, Clarice." Clary just beamed and Father, well, Father, his face slick with sweat, looked radiant as he gazed at Mother. I think they are still after all these years and all the disagreements really very much in love.

June 17, 1917

Cassie says that the crowds are getting rowdier at the picket line. More hecklers yelling insults about how the women are unpatriotic. Mother does not seem in the least disturbed. There are to be new banners made for when a Russian diplomat comes from the new Russian republic. The new republic, they say, is going to grant women in Russia the vote! Harriet wants to go tomorrow to see the Russian diplomat's motorcade arrive at the White House. I would much rather work in the garden. Harriet points out that there will be plenty of time for both, seeing as the garden has just been planted and there has hardly been time for anything to grow yet, including weeds. I guess I'll go.

June 21, 1917

There were huge crowds at the White House gates. The rumors had spread that the suffragists would try something today, a very special demonstration. There were lots of hooligans and roughs in the crowd. One of them turned to me and Harriet and with whiskey-soaked breath said, "I hope you two never grow up to be like them women. It ain't natural." Harriet and I both were simply dumbfounded. We turned to run away but could hardly move because the crowds were so thick. We finally got some distance between us and the loathsome hooligans. We could see the banners that the pickets held. One said, TWENTY MILLION AMERICAN WOMEN ARE DENIED THE RIGHT TO VOTE. RUSSIA, YOU ARE DECEIVED THAT THIS IS A DEMOCRACY! The policemen who for so many months were friendly toward the pickets suddenly looked confused and angry. I was torn between staying and leaving, fearful that something scary might happen.

When Harriet and I both spotted our mothers and Auntie Claire they appeared calm. We dared not wave at them as we usually do for fear of attracting the hooligans' attention, and there were plenty of those around aside from the two we had fled. So many men yelling insults and obscenities. We heard words that were really bad, words that sent creepy shivers through you and made your skin prickle. We finally left before the Russian diplomat ever arrived. We went home to the garden and watered it and checked for any sproutings. It was so peaceful and seemed so far away from all the anger.

LATER

Mother came home and said that there is a rumor that a military zone will be set up around the White House and that there will be a line of guardsmen with drawn bayonets! Not a pretty picture — my mother, Auntie Claire, and Harriet's mother up against the steely points of bayonets.

JUNE 22, 1917

"No!" I screamed out loud, then realized I had been dreaming. I just woke up — woke myself up with this bad dream. It is five minutes to four in the morning. I am writing to try to keep myself calm but my hand shakes so badly that I can barely write. I had the worst nightmare. They say that if you have a dream of falling from a great height you always wake up before you hit the ground. Well, this dream was not about falling but I certainly "hit the ground." I dreamed about those bayonets — shiny, glinting in a hot noonday sun and Mother was walking right up to a guardsman who held one straight out toward her stomach. I was standing to the side crying and begging Mother to "stop walking, please, Mother, just stop." But she didn't. She walked right through the bayonet. Blood spurted out of her, but she would not stop walking. I think I'll go downstairs to the garden. I can't get back to sleep now.

A Few Minutes Later

It is so peaceful here in the garden. I got down on my knees and looked very closely at the rows we had planted. I see some tiny specks of green where we sowed the radish seeds. Little tiny roundish leaves. If fairies had fingernails they would be no bigger than these leaves. I should be happy, so why am I sitting in this garden crying?

JUNE 23, 1917

The first arrests have been made. Lucy Burns and Katherine Morey were arrested late yesterday afternoon by Major Pullman, the chief of police. They had been holding a sign with President Wilson's own words, the ones about WE SHALL FIGHT FOR THE THINGS WE HAVE HELD NEAREST OUR HEARTS. It is not illegal to picket because of something called the Clayton Act. So instead they charged the women with obstructing traffic. Since they were standing quietly on the sidewalk many wonder how this could be. Father says that it will never hold up in court and that they will be immediately released and never brought to trial.

JUNE 25, 1917

Harriet and I took the Ninth Street trolley, the one where Cassie is the conductor. She pretended she didn't know us! Whenever we tried to talk with her she hissed, "I'm on duty. I must not be distracted." I don't see what there is to be distracted from. All she does is take fares and give out transfer tickets. It's not like she is driving an ambulance full of wounded soldiers, which I know she would love to be doing. She was such a bore that we transferred after five blocks.

JUNE 27, 1917

Father was wrong. Ten women have been arrested so far, thank goodness not Mother or Auntie Claire or Harriet's mother. But six of these ten were indeed judged guilty of obstructing traffic, warned of their "unpatriotic and treasonable behavior," and sentenced to pay a twenty-five dollar fine and spend three days in jail.

The women said to the judge that "Not a dollar of your fine will we pay . . . to pay a fine would be an admission of guilt. We are innocent." So they have been sent to jail. I feel that I should write their names down here, to mark them somehow for history although I guess that might seem silly, as their names are printed in the newspaper. But the women are Katherine Morey, Annie Arneil, Mable Vernon, Lavina Dock, Maud Jamison, and Virginia Arnold. They come from Delaware, Pennsylvania, Massachusetts, Virginia, and North Carolina.

Mother says we are having "government by embarrassment." She says that the real crime was not obstructing traffic but embarrassing a president. They say that Wilson was furious with those signs when the Russian diplomats drove through the gates. It is a very odd notion but I think she is right. Mother said that the women of the picket line have always been civil and picketed in a peaceful manner, but that the government has now become uncivil through its efforts to save face and not be embarrassed. But through their uncivil behavior they are the biggest embarrassment of all.

JULY 1, 1917

Unbearably hot. Worked in the garden as long as I could. We now have several rows of fuzzy little green shoots creeping out of the ground. Auntie Claire and Mother and Father went down to the station to see Henry off. He is back from an army training program in Virginia and will sail from New York City for France in less than a week. Barney will probably not have to serve because he has asthma. It was the first time Auntie Claire and Mother and Father had seen Uncle Bayard. Father came home and said they were all "civil" to one another. This word keeps popping up but I think it is a good one and I think about it a lot. I looked it up in the dictionary. The first meaning is "of or pertaining to citizens" and another meaning is "adhering to the norms of politeness and courtesy." I think the meanings are connected. If you are a citizen you are not a slave or a serf. You are a full-fledged member of a society and that means to me that you have to behave in a certain way but that you can also expect a certain behavior from others. I like this word *civil.*

July 2, 1917

I wonder when we will get a letter from either Nell or Alma. They both promised to write. But I suppose it takes a while.

July 4, 1917

Mother was on the picket line but Father drove me and Clary and Harriet out to a spot on the Potomac and we had a picnic in the cool shade and brought our bathing costumes. We changed in the shrubbery and went swimming in a shallow little cove. We had to watch Clary carefully because she does not really know how to swim. But Harriet and I had races. Harriet beat me every time. She is as good at swimming as she is at hockey.

July 9, 1917

Our garden is really coming along. Marietta says we will be able to pick lettuce and radishes in another week.

Cassie told me today that dachshunds are no longer called dachshunds because it is a German word. They are now called Liberty Dogs, and her friend Celia, who also is a streetcar conductor, has one named Fritz and is changing his name to Reginald or Reggie. It will never work. It is very difficult to change a name of an animal or a human. At least if you are a human you can remind people, "Kindly call me Isabel and not Hortense." But if you are a dog, what can you really do about it?

July 11, 1917

At last a letter from Nell!

She began the letter on the ship just as they had entered the war zone, off France, but she was quick to assure us that all had remained absolutely tranquil, even the sea, and that if anything should happen they have all been trained thoroughly, for they have had several drills during the crossing. They line up and divide into groups in front of the particular lifeboat to which they have been assigned. They check each other's life preservers carefully to see if they are buckled properly and so on. All sounded pretty boring until she got to the part about the next evening when they were supposed to meet up with what she called their "escort convoy." The convoy could not find them. The weather kept getting worse and the sea wilder, but by dawn all was well and they met their convoy and she is now stationed in Calais.

Calais, she says, is one of the places where they bring the wounded from the front. They take the wounded into a huge hangar, where they put labels onto the men's cots as to which hospitals they are to be taken to by the ambulances. She has so far just assisted in the sorting out of the wounded, putting the labels on their cots. An ambulance can carry six men at a time. She hopes next week to be assigned to an ambulance. She will not drive one yet, however. Most of the ambulances are driven by British women who are members of a corps called FANY, which stands for First Aid Nursing Yeomanry.

In the evening she spends her time studying a manual on ambulance maintenance. Each team of drivers and their assistants must know how to fix the vehicle if it should break down. She says that Harriet's sister Margaret has been assigned to another field hospital, closer to the front, but that perhaps we should not mention this to the Wilhelms. She says also that there is a girl in her group, Dotty, who was at Radcliffe with Cassie. She adds that there is precious little time for socializing because they are kept so busy. She is thankful that she has not yet seen any wounded suffering from the "ravages of the mustard gas."

The entire time Father was reading the letter Mother just stared into her teacup and occasionally shook her head. Cassie's face was all bright and eager, especially when Father read us the part about two women, Mairi Chrisholm and Baroness Elizabeth de T'Serclaes. Nell says they are the only two women who are actually right at the front. They are very well known and have worked as close as five yards behind the trenches. Mother grew pale as Father read this part, and Cassie brimmed with excitement.

JULY 13, 1917

It was Cassie's day off and she and I were walking to the Ardmore when we ran into her streetcar pal Celia with the dachshund Fritz. Such a cute little fellow and Celia was very nice too. She said calling him Reggie isn't working. I said why not change it to something closer to Fritz like Frenchy or Frankie. Celia's eyes few wide open. "Why, that is sheer genius!" I thought this an overstatement. I mean, it seems so obvious to me that you should change the name to something that sort of sounds like the original one.

JULY 14, 1917

Mother, Auntie Claire, and Mrs. Wilhelm have been arrested! Going with Father to court. Will write more later.

July 17, 1917

I shall never be able to explain this calmly but I am determined to write about it. I want to set down the truth exactly. It is hard to think about the future at times like this, but someday many years from now I want people, maybe my own children, grandchildren, or great-grandchildren, to know the truth. To know how a court of law can become a court of unfairness and senseless punishment and make a joke of justice. Mother and Auntie Claire and Harriet's mother were arrested with a dozen or more other women. It was Bastille Day, the day that celebrates the fall of the French bastille and the French Revolution of 1789. They, along with others, had marched that morning to the White House gates with banners inspired by that revolution, signs with the words LIBERTY, EQUALITY, FRATERNITY. The police were very cunning. Some were on bicycles and some on foot and they would close in on one or two women at a time. But then as soon as they did another woman would step forward and carry the banner closer to the White House gates. I was not there, thank heavens. I did not have to see my mother herded into the police wagon, but Harriet was there and she said all the heckling suddenly stopped and the crowd grew quiet as they bodily picked up one tiny old white-haired grandmother and lifted her into the wagon with the banner. They could not pry her hands loose from it at the courthouse.

I found all this out from Harriet. Then I went with Harriet and Father to the courthouse where Dr. Wilhelm met us. The courtroom was hot and stuffy and smelled bad. There was a one-eyed bailiff. I'll never forget that and he called in a low, growling voice for silence in the courtroom.

Then the sixteen suffragists were led in. They refused lawyers and instead said they would speak on their own behalf. The charges were read and this very skinny, bony-faced man who was the prosecutor and reminded me of a dark bird of prey with his beaked nose and slick black hair began to painstakingly explain how these women obstructed traffic on the sidewalk while taking their banners to the White House gates. One would have thought that they had trucks or immense wagons, whereas they were actually walking single file with the banner held high up and were not obstructing anything. But with his oily words, dramatic pauses, and sideways glances the prosecutor spun a web of lies.

Each woman was allowed to speak in her own defense. I was so proud of Mother. Here is exactly what she said. "While you speak of my obstructing a piece of pavement, a sidewalk, my rights as the citizen of a democracy that through the Clayton Act permits peaceful picketing and demonstration have been undermined as you try to pry a banner from an old lady's hands. What a spectacle this must be for intelligent people, to see a country that claims to be a democracy, and indeed goes to war for democracy in foreign countries where the blood of our sons will be shed, to see the mothers and the grandmothers of these same sons thrown into jail."

And that is exactly what has happened. Mother, Auntie Claire, Mrs. Wilhelm, and thirteen others have been sent to the Occoquan Workhouse, a prison for women in Virginia.

JULY 18, 1917

Father's at a hospital for an emergency. Cassie is working overtime and Mother is in prison. So here I sit — me and my radish! Yes, the first harvest from our little victory garden. I feel utterly defeated and alone. I feel stupid too. Here I was at this big dining room table and Marietta came out, serving me from the platter, mumbling about how she wished people would give her a little more warning before they run off at dinnertime. I, of course, interrupted her muttering and reminded her of the fact that Mother didn't exactly "run off." And she said, "Yeah, and what's I'm to do with all this here chicken and collard greens."

"Don't bring those collard greens anywhere near me," I hissed.

Then she said, "No, you got your radish," and she plunked down some mashed potatoes and a piece of chicken on my plate. "Be back with the spoon bread," she said.

I stared down at the forlorn little radish. It would have been so much fun if Father and Mother and Cassie had been here to celebrate the first vegetable from our garden. To think I was so worried about being orphaned or Mother and Father getting divorced but who would ever have thought of this — Mother in jail. Life is full of awful surprises. Then suddenly I remembered that winter evening when it was just Father and me and that terribly lonely sound of our clinking soup spoons. I stood up, picked up my plate, and walked right into the kitchen. "What's you doin' in here, chile?" Marietta asked.

"I'm not eating in there."

She seemed to understand. In fact, I think Marietta really feels sorry for me. All I ate for dinner was the radish, heaps of spoon bread, and a glass of milk. She didn't even fuss at me about not eating the chicken and mashed potatoes.

I was playing around with the radish on my plate — a little game I had made up kind of like hockey. I was trying to roll it with one scoot of my fork into the rose design on the far edge of the plate. "You gonna fiddle with that radish or eat it?" Marietta asked.

"What's that prison, Occoquan, like?" I asked.

There was a long silence. I looked up slowly from my plate and stared right into Marietta's face. Her eyes met mine. She sighed deeply. She knew I had to know. "First of all it ain't a prison. It's a workhouse."

"Is that not so bad as a prison?"

"I don't know. I never been there. They make them work all the time."

"Are there bars on the windows?"

"I 'spect so."

"Are there murderers, and, you know . . ."

"Mostly colored gals in there. I don't think they done murder. They just poor colored gals who steal or . . ." Her voice dropped off.

"Or what?"

"Would you eat that blasted radish?" Marietta turned and started scrubbing a pot. She had gone huffy on me. I can always tell when she's fed up with my questions. Her shoulders hunch up and she snorts through her nose instead of breathing regularly.

I try to imagine Mother sharing some cell with bars on the windows with colored women. It would be very strange sleeping next to a colored lady.

JULY 19, 1917

Father has tried to go visit but they don't allow visitors for the women yet, and no mail may be received or sent out. Father says this is a violation of a prisoner's rights. He is going to talk to his friend Mr. Abrams, who is an important lawyer.

LATER

Some good news: Harriet said she heard her father say that many important men in Washington have gone directly to the president to protest the imprisonment of the suffragists, including Mr. J. A. H. Hopkins, a close advisor and friend to the president whose wife, Mrs. Hopkins, is imprisoned at Occoquan. Father still is worried to death. Also Dudley Field Malone, a man that everyone says is the president's closest confidante, is trying to organize a protest among the most powerful men in Washington, D.C., and other cities in the Northeast. He is trying to contact John D. Rockefeller!

JULY 20, 1917

There is a rumor of a pardon — yes, that the president will pardon the sixteen women who are imprisoned and that they will be able to go free. They say this is largely Mr. Malone's doing.

July 21, 1917

Must dash — we are going to pick up Mother at Occoquan. She has been pardoned! Will write later.

Later

This is most confusing. Mother and the other women are not exactly pardoned. They refused to allow themselves to be pardoned because they insisted they had nothing to be pardoned for. The president, however, was so embarrassed by having these fine white women in a prison with colored ladies that he forced them to accept the pardon. But it is really as if they are out on bail. They were made to make certain promises. I overhead all this when Mr. Nathan Abrams came over to the house this evening to discuss the case. Alice Paul was there too. Mother was very calm. She was stitching a new purple and gold and white banner. I could not see what it said because I was on my perch on the stair landing. But after everyone had gone I crept downstairs and saw the banner draped over Mother's sewing box. It said, WE DO NOT ASK PARDON FOR OURSELVES BUT JUSTICE FOR ALL AMERICAN WOMEN.

July 22, 1917

Mother was back on the picket line before I was up. She must have left at dawn. How long will it be until she gets arrested again? I don't want to think about it. It's a warm, drizzly day. I think I'll just stay in bed and feel sorry for myself. Started reading *Emma* last night by Jane Austen. For such a bossy girl Emma is very nice.

Oh, nearly forgot to mention that Cassie said that Celia, her friend with the dachshund, said that the new name, Frenchy, is working and to thank me.

July 25, 1917

Worked in the garden in the rain. It felt nice. Marietta kept yelling at me about putting on a raincoat but I like the feel of the rain on my skin. It soaked through my cotton lawn blouse and my hockey bloomers. I took off my shoes and walked barefoot, the mud squishing between my toes. I wish we had had room to plant watermelons. The carrots are ready for pulling. Last week they were no bigger than my middle finger but this week they are much longer. Tomatoes are swelling up, still green, however. I had to go get the stakes Joss had brought over because they are getting so heavy. It started to rain harder, and by the time I came in my hair was plastered down and I was slathered with mud up to my calves.

JULY 28, 1917

At last a letter from Alma and just for me. I am pasting it into my diary. Here it is!

Surrey, England, June 14, 1917

Dearest Kat,

Well, here I am in England working in a hospital in Surrey, not far from London. This is what they call a second-level receiving hospital for the soldiers who have first been treated in a more critical-care one. By the time they get here it is assumed that they will make it. The Red Cross sent me along with five other girls who are also not trained nurses to work with the V.A.D. That stands for Voluntary Aid Detachment. It was formed to provide help to the sick and wounded in case of invasion, but so far, thank God, no invasion. They use us as nurses' aides in hospitals. Our director is the founder of the V.A.D. herself, the countess of Limerick. One would never take her for a countess, however, because she appears so plain in her uniform and wears no makeup and pulls her hair back severely. But to hear her speak is a delight, for she has a lilting Irish accent. And you'll never believe this: She knows that I am not of age and she doesn't even care! She told me that she ran away when she was fourteen with a completely worthless person who drank himself to death by the time she was nineteen. Then she said to me, "You haven't run away. You have run to something, and therein lies all the difference."

There are others like myself who are underage, but as long as we work hard no one seems to care. And we do work hard. My general duties are taking temperatures three times a day, cleaning instruments, and setting up the meds trolleys — meds is what they call medications. I serve the men tea. I am learning about dressings and how to change them. I spend a lot of time lighting their cigarettes. Smoking is permitted when a nurse or aide is in attendance and it seems to be the only solace for many.

Even though I am far from the front I am learning about war. It is frightening. The men are all different but many in some ways are the same. There are the talkers. Talk! Talk! Talk! Not about war but about everything else. "Hey, luv, do you remember the lyrics of that song at the Royal Theatre that Dolly Malone sang? It went something like "If only roses turned blue and stars were green," and whether you remember or not they'll start singing and gabbing about every show they ever saw in London. Or they'll talk about some famous cricket player and some match. Others talk of nothing. They stare wide-eyed all day and often don't even close their eyes at night. It is as if their eyes have been permanently locked open by some horror they have seen. And then some of them are lost in some distant misty memories. There is one fellow, Binker they call him, who was raised in India, and he is always talking about this beautiful garden and his ayah, which I gather is some sort of nursemaid for children, and he talks about a friendly python that lived coiled in a clay jug in the corner of the garden, to which he fed sugar!

This is all so different from Washington. Mother, the picket line, the divorce all seem so far away —

but you don't, Kat. I feel that I can speak more directly to you than anybody else. There are things I simply cannot tell Mother. There are some men with horrible wounds here and there are also men who are mentally very sick. There is a psychiatric wing to the hospital. A man committed suicide last night, and another man is missing half his face. He must be fed through a special kind of straw and tomorrow I am to learn how to do it. I am fearful. I don't know whether I shall manage or not. I must do this. I just must. Their sacrifice is so great and my contribution so little.

Thinking of you, Kat, every minute of every second of every day.

Love, Alma

It is impossible for me to describe my feelings about this letter. Auntie Claire got one too but it was much different.

August 1, 1917

I keep thinking about Alma's letter. I have reread it at least twenty times. I keep wondering whether I would really want to be there. Could I put a straw into the half-blown-away face of a man? Could I look into the locked wide-open eyes of a soldier whose brain is filled with the images of blood and fire and explosions of friends dying and being torn apart? Whenever I think of these things I wind up in the garden — neatening up, weeding, staking tomatoes, sowing another row of lettuce and radishes. It is the only place I can go to drive these awful pictures from my mind.

August 4, 1917

On her days off Cassie has been going over to the National Woman's Party headquarters and working on banners. She encourages Harriet and me to go too, although generally we think it is sort of boring. However, they need all the help they can get, for in a week or so the American envoy to Russia, Mr. Elihu Root, is to return from Moscow and visit the president. So we are to help make signs. The banners say such things as, TO ENVOY ROOT, YOU SAY THAT AMERICA MUST THROW ITS MANHOOD TO THE SUPPORT OF LIBERTY — WHOSE LIBERTY?

While I was stitching on the letters I began to think about how many times I have held fabric between my fingers and stitched the words *America* and *Liberty* since January. Then I think of Alma at the hospital in England. She might at this very moment be holding a different kind of fabric in her hands, winding off bloody bandages as she learns how to dress wounds, listening to tales of a python in a child's garden in India, or hearing the feverish humming of a man trying to recall a prewar ditty from a music hall in London. My fabric is shiny and slick and white, the letters bright purple. I hear the women's voices behind me — Alice Paul dictating a press release, Lucy Burns on the telephone with someone from some congressional committee. I look across at Mother's friend Mrs. Stevens, who is stitching another banner. I can guess the word although she is not yet finished: *kaiser*.

LATER

Mrs. Stevens' banner and many others as well say, KAISER WILSON — HAVE YOU FORGOTTEN HOW YOU SYMPATHIZED WITH THE POOR PUERTO RICANS BECAUSE THEY WERE NOT SELF-GOVERNED? 20,000,000 AMERICAN WOMEN ARE NOT SELF-GOVERNED.

I think this is a little bit scary because there is such a fever to fight the Germans now with men being sent overseas. I am really afraid that if the women carry these signs it could be bad.

AUGUST 6, 1917

I have been thinking every day about those Kaiser Wilson signs. They have not yet begun to carry them. But I think something awful could happen.

AUGUST 8, 1917

I decided to tell Mother how worried I am. When she came in tonight I asked her to please, please, please not carry the sign that says Kaiser Wilson. She folded her hands and stared out the window as she sat on the edge of my bed and said nothing. Then I had an idea. This notion had never crossed my mind before, but the moment I had the idea I knew it had been only a matter of time. I said, "Mother, if you promise not to carry the Kaiser Wilson sign I shall promise not to ever think about going off to the Great War like Alma and Nell."

Mother gave a little gasp and raised her hand to her cheek. Then she set her lips firmly and looked directly at me. "I promise," she said quietly.

AUGUST 10, 1917

It rained today. Rainy days are my favorite for working in the garden. It is just too hot otherwise. Father brought me a poster that he got from a friend of his in the State Department. It shows a lovely lady wrapped in an American flag, striding across a newly plowed field. She is strewing seeds and the writing on the poster says, WILL YOU HAVE A PART IN VICTORY? EVERY GARDEN A MUNITIONS PLANT. I taped it up in my bedroom.

It's not only raining here but it is raining in Belgium in Flanders, where in June the Allied forces had a very successful attack on the Germans near a place called Ypres. Now they have launched another attack. Father explained that this region lies very low and close to the sea and that the constant rains have turned the countryside into a swamp and made air attacks impossible. It is turning into a real catastrophe for the British and French troops. There was a picture in the paper today of a mounted gun with its wheels stuck in the mud and British soldiers pulling on ropes to free it. I keep thinking of Nell and her ambulance and all that mud. How would she ever get an ambulance unstuck?

AUGUST 13, 1917

Father has been following the action in Flanders closely. He says the costs in human lives will be huge and he just shakes his head. In this evening's paper there was a report on a battle on Gheluvelt Ridge, which took place on August 10. It showed wounded men on stretchers. In the corner of the picture I could see the front wheels of an ambulance. It all looked awful. The stretchers with the wounded men were nearly buried in the muck and mud. It reported that as of August 3 more than thirty thousand British soldiers had died in these battles in Flanders.

Tomorrow is the day that the envoy to Russia, Elihu Root, returns to report to the president. This is when the women plan to carry the Kaiser Wilson signs. Mother reassured me that she will not carry a Kaiser Wilson sign, but she will picket as usual.

AUGUST 14–15, MIDNIGHT

What date should I write for this, the worst day of my life?

Yes, I know I said that before, but this is worse. Mother kept her promise and did not carry the Kaiser Wilson sign. I saw that with my own eyes. Harriet and I both went to the White House gates this morning. It now seems years ago. The crowds were very rowdy, and some young navy and army boys began tearing at the banners the women carried. As soon as they would tear one down, however, the women would get another one, as they had several in reserve. But the police would do nothing. They just stood there!

Then President and Mrs. Wilson came driving through the gates. At the same instant two women were knocked to the ground and their banner was torn to shreds. The president and his wife just drove right by. So many banners were destroyed that Harriet and I were sent back to headquarters for more. Soon Lucy Burns and Virginia Arnold and another lady came back to the headquarters with the remaining banners and hung them from the second- and third-floor windows. Well, three sailors got a ladder from the Belasco Theater nearby and leaned it against the building. I heard Lucy Burns cry out, "Oh, my God, here they come." The sailors had scrambled up an iron railing and begun to tear down a banner.

Georgina Sturgis, a friend of Mother's, was on the balcony and asked them to get down. The sailor looked straight at her and then hit her smack in the face. Her lip bled and she stood there simply stunned. The sailor looked stunned too. She said, "Why did you do that?" And he said, "I don't know." Then he tore down the banner and scrambled back down the ladder.

I leaned out the window and yelled, "Coward!"

But Miss Arnold pulled me back in. "It is too danger-ous here for you. Go home."

But it was really too dangerous in the street. So I just stood at the back of the room with Harriet and watched in horror, for we could clearly see Lucy Burns on the bal-cony and two sailors pulling at her. She was swaying back and forth. Miss Burns is very strong and managed to hang on until three or four other women came and pulled her back in. In the meantime we could see eggs and tomatoes being hurled through the air and splatter-ing against the windows. I really don't know how long this went on but suddenly there was a terrible crack. A heavy glass window shattered, and we all realized a bul-let had been fired right into the office and narrowly missed Ella Dean's head. She had been sitting at a desk trying to call the police. Finally the police arrived and broke up the crowds.

As I write, Father is downstairs in his study on the phone with two lawyers. They are arranging the drafting of a resolution to denounce the administration's policy of persecution against women. They are planning mass meetings to condemn the president of the United States, and this time it is not just women who are behind these meetings but men like Father and his lawyer Stuart Walcott and Mr. Abrams.

AUGUST 16, 1917

The pickets will never give up. And the police will never do anything to protect them. Yesterday Miss Elizabeth Stuyversant was hit by a soldier and her blouse torn from her body. Katherine Morey was knocked down and her banner wrenched from her hands, injuring her wrist. Maud Jamison was not only knocked down but also dragged along the sidewalk. Father forbids me and Harriet to go anywhere near the White House now, so who knows what happened today.

LATER

This is what happened today. Mother came back with an ugly purple bruise spread across the entire left side of her face. Someone had hit her. She is not sure who, for she was down on the ground and saw only the person's boots as he tried to kick her but she rolled away. Her skirt is ripped and her stockings are in shreds. It is now said that the administration will begin to arrest pickets tomorrow. But what about the men who punch the women in the face and drag them along the sidewalk?

August 18, 1917

Mother and Mrs. Wilhelm were both arrested once more with four other women. They were sent to Occoquan again. Father is beside himself. Thank goodness Mr. Walcott is here. He keeps saying, "Alfred, let's keep our eye on the ball here." And then he gets on the telephone and rings up the most powerful men he knows — senators, lawyers, millionaires. They propose to have all these powerful men condemn officially the brutal tactics used against the women.

P.S. Thank Goodness Auntie Claire wasn't arrested this time, because Juby and Joss would have their hands full with Clary and the little ones, but Marietta said she would go over and help out if she could. Uncle Bayard comes over occasionally to visit from his men's club. Father says that he thinks this separation has been good, that Uncle Bayard seems a bit more reasonable lately.

August 19, 1917

I did not go to the trial but Cassie did. She said it was a sham. There was nothing mentioned of the awful man-handling of the women by the police officers. The women were sentenced to sixty days in Occoquan. She described the proceedings as absolutely disgusting.

Father and Mr. Walcott continue their struggle and joined with Alice Paul in going right into Congress and pressing representatives to pass a suffrage amendment. Harriet and I now talk about how our fathers are as committed to the cause as our mothers. It seems that the night Mother came home with that terrible bruise on her face that something happened to Father. You could almost see his brain turn over. A fierce light came into his eyes and a curl of disgust at the corners of his mouth. He spat out one single word: "Wilson!" You see, Father does not blame the man who hit Mother, nor does he blame the police. He places the responsibility squarely on the president.

AUGUST 23, 1917

All of the prisoners at Occoquan are being held "incommunicado," which, Father explained, is a fancy word that means cut off from any communication. They can send one letter a month and all incoming mail is censored. Father and Mr. Walcott are working to have them declared political prisoners. I don't quite understand this but I guess if you are a political prisoner it means that you are imprisoned for your beliefs and not because you have stolen or murdered or committed some horrid crime. You therefore are treated better. But I don't know if it would help that much. There are rumors of very bad food and unsanitary conditions.

AUGUST 25, 1917

Harriet and I went to get school things, because we start in a little over a week. Father gave me money for a real good fountain pen. I also bought a simply gorgeous set of colored pencils and vine charcoal, which we shall need for life drawing. We bought notebooks with speckled covers, pencil boxes, and carbon paper, for we are required to make copies of all our essays this year, and we both bought protractors for measuring angles because we shall be doing some geometry. Both Harriet and I are eager for school to begin. The days seem so long and hot and empty. I try to write Mother but it is very difficult to write when you know that your letter is being read by someone else who might ink out a sentence here or there.

August 30, 1917

Our tomatoes have ripened and are absolutely delicious — bright red and juicy and big. Juby brought Clary over this afternoon and we sat on the back steps leading down to the garden. Marietta brought out a shaker of salt and a knife to slice the tomatoes with, but before she could cut the tomato Clary just bit right into it as if it were an apple. Juice squirted all over and it was so funny, but I decided that looked like the tastiest way to eat the tomato so I did the same. I don't think I have ever eaten anything so good, and it was the very best way to eat it. Juby and Marietta were having fits because we were covered in juice and seeds. Our blouses were stained pale red. They were fussing that if we had to do the laundry we wouldn't be eating like a couple of sloppy old pigs.

Then it started to rain softly and I said, "See, God is helping you do the laundry." Juby and Marietta were shocked because they are pretty religious. But Clary and I were still laughing, and I grabbed Clary's hand and we ran out into the middle of the garden and I said, "Do what I do, Clary." I tipped my face up to the rain, for it was coming down harder, and I let the water wash it.

Then we each grabbed another tomato and ate it and got all messy again. Marietta was squawking out the back door at us but Juby pulled her inside and said, "Let 'em be." I think Juby understood how much fun we were having and she knows Clary better than anybody. She knows that because Clary is slow there are not a lot of things she can join other kids in doing, so she was happy for Clary. I was happy not just for Clary, but because I realized that this was perhaps my single happiest moment in months. For ten minutes I did not think of Mother in prison, the picket line, lonely dinners, or missing Alma.

SEPTEMBER 2, 1917

There was a shocking report in the newspaper today, although Father knew about it last night. Senator Lewis Hamilton, from Illinois, made a visit to Occoquan to see two of the imprisoned ladies who are his constituents. He was quoted in the newspaper as being "shocked" and "appalled" at the ladies' appearance. A senator who accompanied him, Gilson Gardner, was quoted as saying, "I have never seen prisoners so badly treated either before or after conviction." Needless to say Father and Cassie and I are worried to death but we are glad this is coming out. Father plans now to go and see his old friend Dudley Field Malone, who is one of President Wilson's closest friends and advisors.

SEPTEMBER 3, 1917

Father took the train to New York today to see Mr. Malone. He holds a job there to which he was appointed by President Wilson. It is a very important job: the collector of the Port of New York City. Father won't come back until tomorrow night. I want to wait up but it is the night before school starts so I really shouldn't.

SEPTEMBER 4, 1917, JUST BEFORE MIDNIGHT

I waited up for Father. I am glad I did. He said Mr. Malone is outraged by the president's actions in regard to the suffragists and called it "the great moral blight on his presidency." I love that phrase. How do people ever think up words like that?

SEPTEMBER 5, 1917

School started today. We have a new Latin teacher. She seems nice. But her name is Miss Trout and I hate to say she sort of looks like one. You know, a puckered mouth and eyes, well, not on the side of her head but pretty far apart. The biggest news is that Miss Janet had a stroke over the summer. I really feel sorry for her. Her mouth is pulled around all funny, and when she speaks it sounds very thick as if her tongue is stirring a heavy batter. She has a brace on one leg and uses a cane. As badly as I feel for her (and I know this is terrible to say but I shall anyway) I hope this means that she cannot tutor me in math if I have problems, which I undoubtedly will. I think I am going to like ancient history a lot. I skipped a little bit ahead in the textbook to the part about ancient Rome.

We have heard very little from Mother. The one letter we received had been so crossed out that there was hardly anything left to read except *Love, Mother* at the end. Every week more women are arrested. They are starting to take them to the city jail in the district. There are rumors that Alice Paul will soon be arrested again.

Cassie went back to Radcliffe today. I think she was actually happy. Her job as a streetcar conductor was starting to bore her. She is all excited about a classics course she will be taking. She made a pile of money, however, and says that she will take Hammy (short for Hamilton), a Harvard buddy of hers, for tea at the Ritz. Her friends have bet her that he will not let her pay.

SEPTEMBER 6, 1917

A letter with a picture from Nell. She looks absolutely dashing in her uniform and is standing in front of her ambulance with a woman named Gwendolyn Battersby, who is the other driver. Nell now drives. Not only that, she is no longer at the hospital in Calais but at Base Hospital Number 21 in Rouen, France. *This is much closer to the front,* she writes. I have decided to paste her letter into my diary. Here it is:

> We travel at night to pick up the wounded, for it is safer under the cover of darkness. The casualties are pouring in from the British offensive at Ypres in Flanders. We have helped set up a dressing station five miles back from the front lines, but now that it is set up we drive the wounded from there to Hospital Number 21. Julia Catherine Stimson is the chief nurse. She is an American from Massachusetts and graduated from Vassar College. She came over in May and is a most amazing person. She has virtually single-handedly set up Hospital 21. When I am not driving I try to help out wherever I can.
>
> Tonight sixty-four men were brought in. We first

give them soup and then take them off to the various wards. Of course, those who must go immediately to the operating theater do. They are tired and dazed and often in terrible pain so we administer morphine. I have learned how to do that — yes, I can now give an injection. One out of every eight casualties needs some sort of amputation. We might have to send for an "emergency group" or surgical team from another unit, as we are quickly becoming overwhelmed with casualties. Today we had fifty-one men to operate on. Yesterday, there were thirty and it looks like more tomorrow.

Keeping ourselves clean is a major problem. We have very little water — just enough to get the mud off the wounded. You cannot imagine how much mud there has been. We have all either cut our hair or if it is really long we wear it twisted up into a knot the Brits call a "pug." I cut mine. It has been chilly recently and many of us have taken to wearing knickerbockers under our uniforms for extra warmth. And we do get cold, especially on our night ambulance runs. Generally our route is from between the dressing station that is attached to Evacuation Hospital Number 8 to Hospital Number 21. At

Number 8 the men's wounds are first dressed and there is a triage system for sorting them out. The gassed men are driven to a gas hospital that specializes in that treatment — mostly for burns, respiratory problems, and blindness. In some of the worst cases, men are actually operated on right there at the evac hospitals, which are mere tents.

We ambulance drivers carry gas masks, helmets, mess kits, and canteens. We have noticed that we are getting more and more gassed men at the evac hospital. I have heard it said that the Germans are getting more desperate and using more and more mustard gas. It is not a pretty sight. It is unbelievably hard work, but it is also difficult to stop to take a rest. The boys suffer so much worse than we do. We barely break to eat, just grab a bit off the mess cart or a cup of tea as it rolls by in the hospital.

I hope all is well with you. I imagine that by the time you receive this letter Kat will be going back to school and Cassie to Radcliffe. Is the picket line still going? Mother and Father, try not to worry about me. I am being as careful as one can in a war zone. Gwen says I have become a wonderful driver in a short time. She comes from Bristol, England, and is a lieu-

tenant in the First Aid Nursing Yeomanry, or FANY.
She has been in FANY since 1914, so she is very ex-
perienced, and most important, smart. She says, and
I am sure this will make you happy, "We do not go in
for heroics. We are judicious in all our actions."
Sometimes this is hard too for we must make a deci-
sion to let a fellow die alone in the mud if it means
risking the ambulance, two drivers, and two stretcher
bearers to pick him up.

Love to you all, Nell

SEPTEMBER 7, 1917

I reread Nell's letter. I cannot believe how boring my life is in comparison. Tonight I must do a Latin translation from Caesar. I must solve for x in ten equations. I must read a chapter on the Fertile Crescent in ancient history while at this very moment Nell is probably administering morphine to some wounded soldier, or driving her ambulance through the night to the evacuation hospital, or soothing a poor gassed fellow in his blistered pain. It seems almost immoral to be reading about the Fertile

Crescent. History sure hasn't taught us much. They say more than thirty thousand men have died in Flanders so far and Lord knows how many in this Great War. What is so "great" about it? Only the numbers of dead and wounded and those forever maimed. Do they call it great because nearly every country under the sun is fighting in it? As if this is some magnificent achievement!

SEPTEMBER 9, 1917

Dudley Field Malone has resigned from his position as collector of the Port of New York City in protest of the administration's treatment of the suffragists.

We are all so excited. To celebrate, Auntie Claire came over with Clary and then Uncle Bayard showed up. He has changed! He seems much softer, and when he saw how happy Clary was to see him together with Auntie Claire, well, I could see tears in his eyes. Oh, I am really hoping, keeping my fingers crossed that things will work out. I refuse to believe that deep down Uncle Bayard is not a loving person who cares deeply for his family.

So things seem better — except when I think of Mother in that awful workhouse, but maybe this will change something. It gives us all hope at least. There is a committee on suffrage in Congress headed by Senator Jones. He has done nothing over the past year, but Auntie Claire said this evening that he is now prepared to make a favorable report to Congress on an amendment to the Constitution. He too visited the workhouse and came away shocked.

SEPTEMBER 12, 1917

The worst thing happened today. Harriet and I were at the Ardmore having a lime rickey when we overheard some women speaking about Occoquan Workhouse. They were saying, "You know, there are rumors that there are worms in the cereal they feed them." Harriet and I both looked at each other and could not take another swallow of our lime rickeys.

SEPTEMBER 14, 1917

The rumors about Occoquan are all true. Women are beaten. The beans, cereal, and rice are all wormy. When they have soup you can see the worms floating on top. All the prisoners drink out of open water buckets. There is no butter, sugar, or milk allowed. There is something called the booby house where difficult prisoners are confined and fed only bread and water. Lucy Burns has just been sent to it because she attempted to talk to an old and frail lady who already was in one of the punishment cells, a Mrs. Kendall. There is only a pail for a toilet in the cells. We learned all of this because one matron, a Mrs. Bovee who was kind toward the prisoners, was fired. She went immediately to the headquarters of the National Woman's Party and made a statement and now it is in all the papers. People are enraged.

Alice Paul has been arrested again. She is in Occoquan while she awaits trial. I think Miss Paul has been arrested at least half a dozen times in her life for the women's suffrage movement, both here and in England, where she was a leader for women trying to get the vote.

SEPTEMBER 19, 1917

Harriet and I both decided that we will write our mothers every day even though it is hard and we know our words will be crossed out. I feel ashamed that I have written only a few times even though they limit the number of letters prisoners can receive. Let Mother see their crossings out. Perhaps she can somehow sense through the ink what I am saying. I have told her some but not all about Nell because I don't want her to worry. I know Father writes her a great deal. I think he gives her practical advice on sanitation and medical matters.

SEPTEMBER 22, 1917

Cassie wrote today that she won her bet. She took Hammy to tea at the Ritz. I have a feeling she might have made something of a scene. Not as bad as the scene she made at the country club when that stupid man said the thing about turning the hose on women.

Feeling kind of achy. Can't write anymore.

OCTOBER 3, 1917

Struck with a terrible cold. I haven't been to school for more than a week. I am way behind in everything. I think

Caesar has conquered all of Gaul by now. It gives me a headache just to think how many translations I'll have to do, although Miss Trout said I shouldn't worry and she'll help me. She is so nice. I want to do well in Latin just because she *is* so nice. I have no real interest in Latin at all. But if I can make Miss Trout happy, well, what's wrong with that? Yes, I know it is not like driving an ambulance through France, filled with bleeding soldiers who have been protecting democracy, but how many avenues are there for a fourteen-year-old girl who is an excellent hockey player but not an especially talented student?

OCTOBER 5, 1917

Mother, Mrs. Wilhelm, Alice Paul, and several others are being sent from Occoquan back to the city jail in the District of Columbia. We read about it in this morning's paper. There was a riot, or what the paper called a mutiny last night at the Occoquan Workhouse. All we know is what we read in the paper and Father says this is not the complete story. He is on the telephone now calling up Mr. Walcott and his friend the superintendent of health for the District of Columbia. What happened according to the paper is that a prisoner, Peggy Johns, a good friend of Mother's, was suddenly being taken out of Occoquan for commitment to a mental hospital. As Father says, "Peggy Johns is one of the sanest people I know. How could they be committing her? This smells of something!" It says in the paper that eighteen women tried to attack the acting superintendent of Occoquan and the matron when they heard of Miss Johns' removal. It was a real brawl. They quote Alice Paul as saying that the women interfered because they were not being told where Miss Johns was being taken and feared that she was to be placed in a punishment cell on bread and water. So now they have removed "the troublemakers" to the city jail. Father says he is going to get to the bottom of this.

OCTOBER 8, 1917

I have by some miracle caught up with my Latin. But now we are supposed to do a term project. It has to be something about ancient Roman civilization — anything, really. Harriet is doing a report on Pompeii and is building a model of the Pompeii forum. I think I am either going to do something on gladiator fighting or the Roman baths.

October 9, 1917

This is the most amazing thing. Celia, the owner of Fritz, now Frenchy — well, today I discovered that her mother is a char lady in the city jail, where Mother is now. I never knew this before and Celia didn't know that Mother was being held there. She thought she was out at Occoquan. Celia says that her mother can smuggle in messages for prisoners as well as take them out. Isn't this wonderful news? I am so excited.

Later

Father is ecstatic about my news of Celia's mother. He says we must invite Celia over for dinner. Celia and I had planned to meet tomorrow at the Ardmore. And Father and I shall have letters ready for her to take.

October 11, 1917

We delivered our letters to Celia yesterday at the Ardmore. Harriet came with me for she had letters from herself and her father for Mrs. Wilhelm. It was definitely too chilly for lime rickeys. We're in the ice cream soda season. It made me think of Alma. I haven't heard from her since the first letter. I would be more worried but at least she, unlike Nell, is in England and out of the war zone.

October 12, 1917

Hooray! A letter from Alma. I can hardly believe it came just when I was thinking so much about her. She has been switched to another hospital in the north of England. It specializes in gassed patients. She says that there is one fellow, a double amputee who is also now blind, with whom she has become close and she spends quite a bit of time reading aloud to him. She says he is really quite handsome despite the scarring from the gas. He was a student at Cambridge University in England before the war, studying astrophysics. She writes, "It is so sad. Cyril is incredibly smart but now he cannot read his beloved physics texts, so I try the best I can. It is difficult, and to think he cannot even see the stars now." She says some of his vision might come back.

OCTOBER 15, 1917

I finally decided on a term project for Latin. I am doing chariot racing and am calling my report *Panem et Circenses,* which translates to Bread and Circuses. What the expression really has come to mean is those citizens who give away important rights in exchange for material pleasures. A first-century Roman named Juvenal wrote about all this (unfortunately in Latin, which is taking me forever to translate). He said the Romans were so wild for chariot racing that they cared about nothing else, or something like that, and they gave up certain rights. I thought I would try to relate it to the suffrage movement. But the women haven't exactly given up anything, for they never had the vote to begin with and there certainly is no chariot racing around Washington or anyplace else I have heard of. Oh, well, I'll figure out something to say in this report.

OCTOBER 17, 1917

A letter from Mother! A real uncensored letter. I am pasting it right here.

Dearest Family,

Greetings from cell 21, second tier. Things here in the city jail are not quite so awful as they were at Occoquan. So far no worms in the cereal. The prison warden, Mr. Zinkham, is at least human, which is a great improvement over that beast at Occoquan, Superintendent Whittaker. Mr. Zinkham has actually said that he wishes the police commissioner would allow us to be treated as political prisoners. Father will be pleased to know (well, I am not sure if pleased is the right word) that the wife of his old friend from the Public Health Service, Harvey Wiley, is in the cell next to mine. She is doing as well as can be expected, as am I too. I have had a rash on my left arm and I pick all the lice I can out of my hair. I sleep and I think. We are not permitted any reading or writing materials, but one kind soul has sneaked in this pencil and paper. I am not in despair but I am in a quandary. I wonder constantly how this could be happening. How can President Wilson countenance this treatment of all these good American women, law-abiding American women who in fact only want to participate wholly in a democracy? We have so much to contribute. Why abuse us and attempt to denigrate our cause and humiliate us? Note I say "try," for I am sure that the president ultimately humiliates only himself and his administration. No matter what achievements are ahead this will be a dark stain on his legacy as president of the United States.

Know that I think of each of you every minute of every hour of every day. My dearest Kat, I hate that I am missing so much of these very important months of your life. Yours and Father's sacrifice is perhaps the greatest in our family — that of the youngest child and the patient and understanding husband. But you both know why I do this. Fear not, I have no despair. I remember the words of Ralph Waldo Emerson: "God offers everyone his choice between truth and repose. Take which you please — you can never have both." We Bowens are all truth seekers. So there is consequently little repose in sight for now.

Love, Mother

October 30, 1917

I haven't had any time to write in my diary, between my chariot racing report, hockey practice, and writing Mother. It is so much easier to write her now that I am sure the letters aren't being censored. I mostly tell her everything I am doing. In addition, I have taken to reading the papers very carefully so I can report on the war and also any articles on the suffrage movement.

October 31, 1917

Clary came over and carved pumpkins with me for Halloween. We set out dishes of candy to hand out to trick-or-treaters. I made Clary a crown from tinfoil and got some old silk fringed shawls of Mother's and dressed her up like a princess. I got myself a sheet, which I draped toga-style, and then pulled some ivy growing on the side of the house and made myself a wreath. I am that Roman fellow Juvenal who wrote about the chariot racing. Father took our pictures.

November 3, 1917

The Sixty-fifth Congress of the United States of America, known as the War Congress, adjourned three days ago. Here is what they found time to accomplish: They appropriated forty-seven million dollars for the dredging of rivers and harbors, they passed a law to protect migratory birds, and they voted to establish more federal judgeships. But there was not one bit of action on the suffrage amendment. Alice Paul, who was out on bail and awaiting her trial, led a group to the White House to protest against letting the lawmakers go home. Well, now she is back in jail.

P.S. There was a picture in the paper today of an antisuffrage march in New York showing two women (!!) carrying a sign that says, NEW YORK STATE DENIES THE VOTE TO CRIMINALS, LUNATICS, IDIOTS, & WOMEN. Can you imagine two women agreeing to carry such a sign?

November 4, 1917

Here is what Alice Paul said at her trial: "We are being imprisoned not because we obstructed traffic, but because we pointed out to the president the fact that he was obstructing the cause of democracy at home while Americans were fighting for it abroad."

Well, they gave Alice Paul a seven-month sentence! That is the longest sentence ever given. People are up in arms. She has been put in solitary confinement. There are rumors that she might begin a hunger strike and that others will follow. I cannot bear to think of this. I pray that Mother will not join the hunger strike. She has been imprisoned for so long now that I don't think she would last if she began to starve herself. I am completely depressed.

November 6, 1917

I saw Celia today and she said her mother told her an interesting story about Alice Paul in jail. The jail is very stuffy and airless and Alice Paul looked up and asked the matron why a high window wasn't opened. The matron said if they opened it, it would let a draft in and they would have to give more clothes to the colored prisoners. Alice Paul just snorted and went to pull on the rope that would open the window. Guards came and yanked the rope from her hands, but in her pocket she always carries a book of the verses of the English poet Robert Browning, and she turned and heaved the book toward the window. She was right on target. Yes, bull's-eye and the window broke, letting in fresh air. Miss Paul would probably make an excellent hockey player.

NOVEMBER 7, 1917

Flunked a test on binomial expansions.

NOVEMBER 8, 1917

Did really awful on an ancient history test.

November 9, 1917

Miss Pruitt called me into her office and said that teachers have reported that I am inattentive and seem distracted. She asked if something was troubling me. Is something troubling me? That is the understatement of the century. I just broke down in tears and said, "Yes something is, as a matter of fact. My mother is probably going to starve herself to death in prison." Miss Pruitt's eyes became misty and she stepped around her desk and hugged me. It was like hugging an ironing board. She is very flat and stiff. But I couldn't stop crying. I really want my mother back. I cannot stand to think of her growing thinner and thinner every day in cell 21, second tier.

November 10, 1917

The longest picket line ever was at the White House today to protest Alice Paul's sentence. Harriet had a cold and didn't go but I went and met Celia there. She asked me if I had any messages for Mother. Suddenly I had an idea. Could Celia's mother somehow sneak me onto the prison grounds and perhaps to a spot where at least I might be able to see my mother from her cell? I know that she does have a cell with a window. Because she wrote about seeing the sky and how "reading" cloud pictures is the only reading allowed. Celia said she thought it might be done. She will come by my house tomorrow after school.

November 11, 1917

Guess what? Lunatics, idiots, and criminals did not get the vote in New York BUT women did. The state of New York with more people than any state in the Northeast is now a women's suffrage state. It was passed with a referendum vote. This is really good news. Father says it is really going to put the pressure on President Wilson and Congress to pass an amendment.

November 12, 1917

I have seen Mother. Celia came around just as she promised. She brought with her a great gray overcoat in which she wrapped me up, and slapped a hat on my head. We then took the number 24 trolley, switched to the 25, and stepped off in front of the city jail. Celia had alerted her mother, who met us at a gate. She led us past two guards. It was dusk and I stood at the edge of a courtyard sliced by the shadow of a tall chimney. Celia's mother told me to look up at the nearest corner and that Mother would be standing there in a few minutes. It was chilly and that time of evening when everything seems to be darkening into shades of gray, as if all color is being drained from the world. Then suddenly within all this gray I looked up and saw white. It was Mother's face at the barred window. It was a shock. I almost did not recognize her. It seemed skeletal, her forehead very large and bony. Most shocking of all, her hair was white at the temples. Celia gave me a little nudge so I would step out from the shadow of the chimney. I did, and I took off my hat so she could see me. I raised my hand at the very same instant Mother raised hers. "Mother!" I whispered. I saw my name form on her lips. "I'm all right, Mother. We miss you." Just then we heard a guard and Celia pulled me back into the shadows and Mother's face disappeared — extinguished like a small flame.

November 15, 1917

I wrote a letter to President Wilson today and delivered it to the White House gate. A guard patted me on the head and smiled and said, "Sure, I'll see that it gets right into the president's hands." I am not so sure but it made me feel good writing it. Here is what I wrote.

Dear Mr. President,

I am a fourteen-year-old American girl and my mother has been a picket. I have not seen her in more than two months. I have not been able to tell her that I flunked my test on binomial expansions or got an A on a Latin exam. I have not been able to tell her about certain physical changes in me and I need to ask her some questions because it is simply too embarrassing to ask my father even though he is a doctor. I was not able to carve a pumpkin with my mother this year for Halloween as I had every Halloween since I can remember. I have not been able to enjoy any of the "inalienable rights" as spoken of in the Bill of Rights because you have imprisoned my mother.

Now, I know you will probably say it is her own fault.

She deprives herself of these joys and responsibilities of motherhood through her own stubbornness. Let me just ask you one simple question: What is so scary about women voting? I think in your stubbornness you have become a kidnapper of sorts — a kidnapper of my mother. I am sorry to put it so bluntly, but this is the truth.

Respectfully,

Kathleen Grace Bowen

NOVEMBER 17, 1917

The hunger strike in the city jail has begun, led by Alice Paul. I am sure Mother is joining it.

NOVEMBER 19, 1917

A message from Mother today. Yes, as I thought, she has joined the hunger strike. She writes that she along with everyone else on her tier is refusing food.

November 24, 1917

There is a terrible rumor that both Alice Paul and Lucy Burns are close to death. I cannot bear to think or write anymore.

November 25, 1917

Of all the stupid things, I have won the Latin Term Prize! This seems so ridiculous considering what is actually going on in my life. There is to be a ceremony where I get the award at the annual holiday open house. I didn't even want to go to the dumb open house. I am dreading it because with Mother in jail it will be so awkward. I think I went overboard when I started thinking about how much pleasure my doing well in Latin would give poor old Miss Trout. I didn't think about poor old me.

November 26, 1917

Another message from Mother:

> *I am all right. I feel quite weak but I have not fainted as some have. They have taken Alice Paul to a psychiatric ward where they threaten to force-feed her.*

I know this is wrong for me to say but I wish they would do that to Mother. I don't want her to die. She cannot die.

November 27, 1917

They have force-fed Mother as well as Mrs. Wilhelm. Mrs. Wilhelm wrote and said it was the worst experience of her life. They stuff a tube down your throat. It hurts and then they pour down liquids with beaten eggs. They poured it in so fast that she gagged. Father looks like a zombie. Tonight he said, "I cannot believe that we are living in America, within the shadow of the White House."

We have decided not to have a Thanksgiving celebration this year. It seems wrong to sit down to a feast when women are starving themselves. The Walcotts invited us but Father declined. He asked that Marietta just make some soup and corn bread. That's fine with me.

November 28, 1917

The pickets still picket and the police still arrest them. The news is out about the hunger strike, and it is said the hunger strike is spreading to other jails where suffragists are held.

Later

Finally had a bit of inspiration for my Latin speech for the award ceremony. I was sitting in Father's study at his desk using the big dictionary when there it was, staring me in the face. His degree from Dartmouth College with the college motto *Vox Clamantis in Deserto,* which means a voice crying in the wilderness, or I think it can mean shout or cry in the wilderness. I asked Father about it and he said that because Dartmouth College was started in the wilderness area of New Hampshire with a charter originally to bring education to the Indians that this is the reason for the motto. Well, I think it might make a good idea on which to base my speech. I can talk about my *mater,* Mother, and Harriet's *mater* and every other woman who has picketed and is now imprisoned for suffrage as voices in the wilderness.

November 29, 1917

Mother is now in the psychiatric ward. That is where they put most of them for force-feeding but she sill manages to sneak out messages. She said that Dr. Gannon, who is in charge of the force-feeding, is the most hated man in the entire prison, for he comes in "waving his tubes" and jugs of liquid and often calls them Missy and then says, "I will show you who rules this place. You women think you do. But I will show you that you are wrong."

Father is furious. He has gone to the district board of health and is filing a complaint. He called Mr. Walcott and plans a suit and is going to try to get Dr. Gannon's license revoked for violation of his Hippocratic oath and "gross and inhuman conduct" unbecoming to a physician.

November 30, 1917

There are actually rumors that all the women might be released from jail. I dare not think or even hope. Harriet and I went to the Ardmore and made a pact that we would not speak a single word about it for fear of jinxing it. So this is the last you will hear of it from me.

December 1, 1917

More stupidity. I am to be an angel in the Christmas pageant. I so wanted to avoid being onstage this year. If I could only have lurked in the chorus or at best been a shepherd. Shepherds really have very little to do. You sleep at stage left in a heap of smelly old cheesecloth robes with fabric tied around your head Arab-style. Then when the chorus sings, "Shepherds, shake off your drowsy sleep" you get up and lumber across the stage and look at the baby Jesus — this raggedly old doll in a manger. Posy Elder, the clomp-like-an-elephant hockey player, is the Virgin Mary. She is a better Virgin Mary than she is a hockey player, I'll tell you that. We would have won the last game of the season if she had not completely missed the puck the single time it was passed to her. Anyhow, being an angel is awful. There are three of them and you must stand on this raised platform under hot lights in these satin robes and raise your eyes toward heaven.

DECEMBER 2, 1917

A letter from Alma. I think she might be falling in love with that fellow with no legs that she has been reading to in the hospital. Everything is Cyril this and Cyril that. I know this sounds absolutely terrible and I would only write it here in this diary but I cannot imagine falling in love with someone who does not have legs. I mean, he would have to have a simply fabulously great personality. I know I am a narrow type.

I finished my Latin speech. It is only thirty-five words. I had to rehearse it with Miss Trout. She beamed. Tomorrow night is the holiday open house where I shall be presented with the award. Harriet is getting one for being captain of the hockey team. Susannah Fedders is getting one for proficiency in math.

But none of the other winners has to do anything

special. Oh, yes, Lilabeth Morse won in French and she does have to say something in French.

December 3, 1917

I am so furious. Father has been called away on an emergency so he cannot come to the holiday open house this evening at seven. I have to go with Marietta, and Joss shall drive us. I didn't want to get this dumb award in the first place and now I have to go all by myself. Well, Marietta counts but she's not a parent. This is an open house for parents. Harriet's father will be there. Here I am, a virtual orphan. And the holiday season about to start. Where are you, Charles Dickens?

December 4, 1917, Just After Midnight

I can hardly write I am so unbearably happy. Mother is back! That is why Father and Harriet's father could not attend the open house. All of the women prisoners were released. The president knew that the women were unswerving and would starve themselves to death and if they did he would have to bear the consequences. So here is how it happened.

I was third in line to get my award. Harriet had already received hers as well as Susannah Fedders for math. I was wearing my nice blue velvet dress with the hand-crocheted collar and a cameo at the neck that had belonged to my Grandmother Bowen. I had my speech gripped in my hand. I didn't think I would have to look at it, I hoped, for I had said it about thirty-five thousand times in the last two days. Anyhow, Miss Pruitt was on the platform and she was saying, "And now for the Cornelia Alder Bennet award for proficiency in Latin and exhibiting a true appreciation of that ancient culture, Miss Kathleen Bowen." Right before she announced my name I heard the doors creak at the back of the auditorium. I didn't pay much attention, for people were constantly taking little kids out who whined or had to go to the bathroom. I got to the platform and received the scroll with my name in gold letters, and then just as Miss Trout told me to do I turned and faced the audience, took a breath, and counted to three before beginning my speech. But then in the back instead of Marietta I saw the tall figure of my father. *So his emergency is over,* I thought, but suddenly the breath I was taking locked in my throat, for next to him, her face as pale as a lick of white flame, was my mother. I opened my mouth and instead of the words *Vox Clamantis in Deserto* there was a shriek, a cry in that auditorium and the wilderness of the last months dissolved. I jumped from the platform and tore down the aisle. MOTHER! MOTHER! I was screaming. And then Harriet spotted her mother too and it was all pandemonium as everyone in the auditorium burst into cheers and hoorays. I ran to Mother and flung my arms around her. I think I actually picked her up. "Mother, Mother, you're free! You are free!"

And she was so different. Her hair was almost all white and I could feel her bones. We kept holding each other away so we could see each other. It was as if we were drinking in each other's face. It was a miracle — my own mother not dead but alive and before me. I remember having one fleeting thought, which was that I must have grown so much taller, that I never knew how much I'd grown until I measured myself against my mother. Nonetheless when I hugged her again and looked down at her thin white hair I knew that I hugged a giant and that I would still have to grow in ways that could not be measured in inches.

EPILOGUE

Kathleen Bowen's mother was never imprisoned again, although she continued to work fearlessly for suffrage. Within the next few months the Bowen family was struck by a deep tragedy. The influenza epidemic of 1918 had just begun to break out and Cassie Bowen, who was at Radcliffe, became sick one night and by the next morning was in a coma. She died a few days later. The epidemic, the worst one in history, killed more than twenty million people throughout the world. Miss Pruitt's Academy shut its doors for most of the winter and spring term of 1918. Miss Pruitt's elderly sister Miss Janet died of the illness. Posy Elder, however, was the only student from Miss Pruitt's who succumbed to the influenza.

Far away in Europe the flu raged as well, but Nell continued to drive her ambulance through the mud behind the lines of war-torn France. She returned at the end of the war in 1918 after the armistice and entered medical school. Alma never returned. She indeed had fallen in love with Cyril Eddington. When she was eighteen they married and she became the Duchess of Eddington. Kat and her family and Alma's family, including her father, who had since reconciled with Auntie Claire, sailed over together for the wedding at the Eddington family estate, Stoke March. Kat and Clary were bridesmaids. Alma continued her work with the Red Cross and the Voluntary Aid Detachment in England.

After the wedding Kat returned to the United States to begin her studies at Radcliffe College. She majored in classics and became fascinated with archeology. In 1922 in the Valley of the Kings in Egypt the tomb of King Tutankhamen had been discovered by Egyptologist Howard Carter. Excavations for this tomb were to go on for several years. Kat tried to get on the excavation team but was refused, because women were not permitted as official team members. She decided to try her luck going as a journalist to cover the exciting discovery for the *Boston Globe.* So impressed was Howard Carter with her thorough presentation that he invited her to examine a few small artifacts and write them up as a monograph for a scholarly journal. Once more Kat Bowen impressed him with her scholarship, insight, and good writing. Finally, Carter appealed to Lady Carnavon, the benefactor and supporter of the project, and requested that a small stipend be given so Miss Kathleen Bowen could work through the following field season. Kat became one of the most important team members in the excavation of the burial chamber.

She dropped out of Radcliffe for a year and a half to work on King Tut's tomb, but then returned to graduate with honors in 1926. She went on to get a graduate degree in archeology and on another dig in Egypt met her future husband when she was bitten by a cobra and nearly died. Her husband, Dr. Solomon Gershon, was in a group of tourists and immediately knew what to do to prevent shock and heart seizure. She was rushed to the nearest medical station and administered a potent anti-venom drug. Kat lingered in a coma for almost a week and Solomon, intrigued by this unique and daring young American woman, fell in love with her. It took Kat a little longer. Gershon told her it was love at first sight, but as Kat reminded him, she was in a coma with her eyes closed, so she needed a little more time. They married two years later.

The Bowen-Gershons, as they became known, settled in New York, where Solomon practiced medicine and Kat took a position at Barnard College as a professor of classics and archeology. They had three children — all girls — one named Cassandra. It was Cassandra to whom Kat gave the diary. Cassandra in turn typed it with carbon sheets and gave it to each of her four daughters and to her one son.

Kat had become president of the League of Women Voters in New York City and continued her mother's fight for women's rights until her death this past year. On her gravestone she requested only her name and the phrase "Ain't I a woman?"

LIFE IN AMERICA
IN 1917

HISTORICAL NOTE

Athough Kat's mother, Eleanor Bowen, is a fictional character, she followed in the steps of some very real people who began fighting for women's rights in the middle of the nineteenth century — women such as Susan B. Anthony and Elizabeth Cady Stanton, who are credited with the founding of the women's movement. These women fought not only for the ballot but also against other terrible inequalities that perhaps are unimaginable to young readers today.

For example, it was unlawful for a woman to sue for damages. In 1873, a woman in Massachusetts slipped on the ice and injured herself. She could not sue, but her husband was awarded thirteen hundred dollars as compensation for *his* loss of her ability to work. It was easy perhaps to speak of men being gallant and chivalrous, but fine manners gave women no protection in the eyes of the law. They could not vote. They could not get mortgages. They could not sue in a court of law. They had limited rights of property, and they were often prevented from pursuing higher education.

In 1848, Elizabeth Cady Stanton, a housewife and mother of several children, became very angry about the status of women in America. She decided she had to do something to effect a change. One day Mrs. Stanton began reading the Declaration of Independence aloud to herself and an idea was born. Wherever she could she inserted the word *women* into this document. For example, "We hold these truths to be self-evident, that all men and women are created equal."

Mrs. Stanton decided to have a meeting, a convention for women at which women's rights could be discussed. The meeting was held in her hometown of Seneca Falls, New York, in 1848. Elizabeth and her good friend Lucretia Mott, a Quaker and abolitionist, planned this conference. Elizabeth had met Lucretia because her own husband, Henry Stanton, was a leader in the abolitionist movement. More than three hundred women and some forty men attended that first meeting in July 1848. Among the men was the former slave and great abolitionist Frederick Douglass. It quickly became apparent that the rights of women and the antislavery movement had a lot in common.

A Declaration of Principles was signed at the meeting and a resolution was passed, affirming the right of women to vote. The conference at Seneca Falls is generally thought of as the beginning of the women's movement in America.

The movement began to grow rapidly. During the 1850s some sort of women's rights convention was held almost every year. At a women's convention in Akron, Ohio, a former slave, Sojourner Truth, stood up to respond to some men who had been ridiculing women. She was furious, and although she had never learned to read or write, she gave one of the most stirring speeches in the history of the women's movement when she asked the question, "Ain't I a woman?"

"Look at my arm! I have ploughed and planted, and gathered into barns, and no man could head me — ain't I a woman? I could work as much and eat as much as a man — when I could get it — and bear the lash as well! And ain't I a woman? I have borne thirteen children, and seen most all sold to slavery, and when I cried out with my mother's grief, none but Jesus heard me — and ain't I a woman?"

Other leaders began to emerge. Lucy Stone, a magnificent orator, became head of the American Woman

Suffrage Association (AWSA). Perhaps the greatest of all was Susan B. Anthony. She and Elizabeth Cady Stanton became the two leaders of the National Woman Suffrage Association (NWSA). Anthony organized women to go door to door in the state of New York to gather signatures to submit to the state legislature for three reforms: the right of women to control their own earnings, the right to be the legal guardians of their own children, and the right to vote. There were six thousand signatures on the petition but the state judiciary committee told her that was not enough. So she began again on Christmas Day of 1854 to get more. She went to countless towns, gave innumerable speeches, and distributed literature and petitions concerning women's rights. At one point her feet became frostbitten in the bitter cold and she had to be carried onto the stage for her speech. Eventually she collected four hundred thousand signatures and had raised more than three thousand dollars for the Union effort in the Civil War. In 1872, Susan B. Anthony voted in Rochester, New York, and was arrested and prosecuted for voting illegally. Voting would not become legal until November 1917, when New York became a suffrage state, giving women the right to vote. The western states, however, moved more quickly.

In 1869, the Wyoming Territory adopted women's suffrage and in 1890, became the first state admitted to the Union as a suffrage state. During the 1890s Colorado, Idaho, and Utah entered the union as suffrage states. The efforts of women in the East were, however, undaunted. The two associations, one led by Susan B. Anthony and Elizabeth Cady Stanton and the other by Lucy Stone, eventually merged into a new group called the National American Woman Suffrage Association (NAWSA). A new leader was emerging. Much younger than Susan B. Anthony or Elizabeth Stanton, Carrie Chapman Catt was incisive and politically minded. She set out a plan at the annual convention of the NAWSA that coordinated the national, state, and local branches of the association in their efforts. She also organized a finance committee. Mrs. Catt became the head of the Organization Committee and of the NAWSA and in 1900, upon Susan B. Anthony's retirement, became president of the association. She made sure that every single state and territory in the union was brought into the National-American. In 1910, Washington was won as a women's suffrage state, and by the following year California had passed suffrage.

In 1912, Alice Paul, who had earned a Ph.D. in social

work, had just returned from England, where she had been studying firsthand the conditions in British tenements and the work of settlement houses, or charity homes, for orphans and poor people. She became involved in suffrage in England and then returned to the United States to Washington, D.C., to work on a federal amendment for women's suffrage. Just as Susan B. Anthony and Elizabeth Cady Stanton became a team, so did Alice Paul and Lucy Burns, who had also just arrived in Washington. Together they founded the Congressional Union for Woman's Suffrage and later the National Woman's Party. They led many demonstrations in Washington, which already had several women's suffrage clubs, and with the help of the millionaire Mrs. O. H. P. Belmont, were able to establish the headquarters of their party in the Cameron House, a mansion across Lafayette Square from the White House. Alice Paul was a great publicist. She organized not only demonstrations in Washington but also in 1915 arranged a motor caravan from San Francisco to Washington that carried a suffrage petition that was eighteen thousand feet long and bearing half a million names.

However, it was in 1917 that she gained the most press attention when she organized the silent vigil of the

Woman's Party pickets at the White House. During this time more than two hundred women were arrested in violation of their civil rights as defined by the First Amendment of the Bill of Rights, which guarantees freedom of speech, and the Clayton Act, which made it lawful for any American to demonstrate. The women were incarcerated and treated brutally. The truth about this treatment was revealed by a former matron, Mrs. Virginia Bovee, who had worked at Occoquan. A hunger strike began in November of that year, and by December 3 all remaining prisoners were released. Other smaller incidents, such as when Cassie asked for the attorney general's resignation, were based on fact. Mr. Gregory, the attorney general at that time, really did suggest that hoses be turned on the women to make them look ridiculous. The August riots in which the women were attacked by young Army and Navy men and during which the three men scaled the wall of the headquarters building and nearly pulled Lucy Burns off the balcony really did happen. A shot was fired at that time into the headquarters, narrowly missing Ella Dean.

By the end of 1917, six states had won the right for women to vote. In fact, by the end of that year the number of presidential electoral votes in which women had a share was 215. The pressure was on. Within days after the release of the women from Occoquan and the Washington, D.C., city jail, committees in Congress began acting on the suffrage amendment. They went to President Wilson, who finally agreed to a date for a vote on the amendment. The House of Representatives agreed to vote on the suffrage Amendment on January 10, 1918. The Nineteenth Amendment passed in the House of Representatives but did not pass in the U.S. Senate until 1919. Finally in 1920, the Nineteenth Amendment was ratified by two-thirds of the states, and American women gained the vote.

In anticipation of the passage of the amendment, Carrie Catt in 1919 formed a new organization called the League of Women Voters to make sure that women really did get out and vote once they had the right. The league also taught citizenship classes in schools, and on election days they would baby-sit and provide rides to the polls for women.

The story, however, of women's rights was and is far from over. In the 1960s and 1970s, the women's movement found vigorous new leaders who fought for issues such as equal pay, better birth control methods, and equal opportunities in the workplace. The National

Organization for Women was founded by Betty Friedan. Gloria Steinem, a journalist, and Kate Millet, a scholar, were among many women who wrote extensively on the subject of feminism. Although many good bills and laws were passed, such as the Equal Pay Act of 1964, the Equal Rights Amendment failed to win ratification, to the disappointment of many American women. Women today continue to struggle to gain and protect those rights that Elizabeth Cady Stanton whispered to herself as she reread the Declaration of Independence in her home in Seneca Falls, New York, in 1848.

Despite the fact that the world was at war and the women's suffrage movement was in full force, daily life in Washington, D.C., was quite ordinary. On any given day, two young girls might stop to share a soda at the local fountain on their way home from school.

President Woodrow Wilson and his wife, Ellen Axson Wilson, did not support the women's suffrage movement until 1918.

Sojourner Truth, a former slave, was an advocate for the abolition of slavery and for women's suffrage. Her famous speech, delivered in 1851 in Akron, Ohio, mocked the idea that women were inferior to men: "Look at me, I have plowed and planted . . . and ain't I a woman? Sisters, if women want any rights, more than they got, why don't they just take them, and not be talking about it?"

Elizabeth Cady Stanton, a housewife and mother who decided that the rights promised to "all men" in the Declaration of Independence must also be extended to women, convened the first women's rights conference in 1848 in Seneca Falls, New York. The ideas discussed at this meeting laid the foundation for the women's suffrage movement.

Mrs. Oliver H. P. Belmont used her wealth to further the suffragettes' cause. She bought the Cameron House, a mansion located across the street from the White House, to serve as the Woman's Party headquarters.

Alice Paul fought for women's rights first in England, and then again upon her return to the United States. She led demonstrations all over the country and carried an 18,000-foot-long petition bearing over half a million signatures supporting women's right to vote. In this photograph she is sewing a banner for a vigil.

The National Woman's Party organized a silent vigil in front of the White House in 1917. They picketed through snow and all kinds of unfavorable elements for over nine months.

More than 200 women picketers were arrested in 1917. In violation of their civil rights, they were tried and found guilty on trumped-up charges of obstructing traffic. In prison, the women were forced to endure terrible conditions and harsh treatment.

Lucy Burns, one of the leaders of the women's suffrage movement, was among those incarcerated in 1917 for picketing. A fiery orator, she organized demonstrations all over the nation. She led many of the women prisoners in a hunger strike that eventually led to their pardons and release from jail.

While the women's suffrage movement heated up on the homefront, World War I raged in Europe. Voluntary Aid Detachment Ambulances were manned by Boy Scouts and volunteer nurses. They often drove to the battlegrounds and transported injured soldiers to various field hospitals. The pioneering work these women did contributed to the women's equal rights movement.

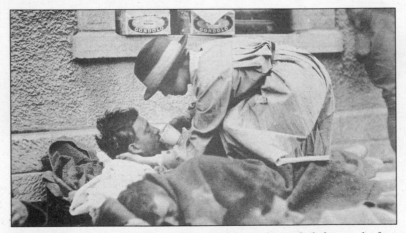

Women who volunteered for the American Red Cross also worked close to the front lines. They often put their own lives in danger while helping to save the lives of soldiers and administering to the sick and wounded.

Leaders of the suffrage movement, Mrs. Carrie Chapman Catt and Miss Mary Garrett Hay, finally cast their ballots for president of the United States at a poll in New York City in 1920.

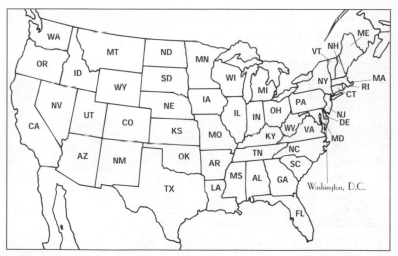

This modern map shows the approximate location of Washington, D.C.

A Timeline of American Women in Politics

1828: Isabella Bonfree, a slave, a feminist, and an abolitionist, is freed. She later takes the name Sojourner Truth and begins to preach against slavery.

1837: The first National Female Anti-Slavery Society convention, organized by Lucretia Mott, meets in New York City.

1838: In speaking to the Massachusetts legislature about the cruelty of racial prejudice, Angelina Grimke becomes the first woman in the United States to address a lawmaking body.

1848: The first women's rights convention is held in Seneca Falls, New York, where the "Declaration of Sentiments and Resolutions" is adopted.

1869: National Woman Suffrage Association is created by Susan B. Anthony and Elizabeth Cady Stanton.

1872: Thirteen women, including Susan B. Anthony, are permitted to vote after arguing that the Fifteenth Amendment gave them the right. They were later arrested and fined.

1913: Alice Paul and Lucy Burns organize the Congressional Union, which later became known as the National Woman's Party.

1917: Jeanette Rankin of Montana is the first woman elected to serve in the United States House of Representatives.

1918: President Woodrow Wilson changes his stance on women's suffrage and delivers a speech to the United States Senate in support of a constitutional amendment allowing women the right to vote.

1920: The Nineteenth Amendment is passed on August 26, granting women the right to vote.

1924: Nellie Tayloe Ross of Wyoming becomes the first woman elected governor of a state.

1932: Hattie Wyatt Caraway is the first woman elected to the U.S. Senate. She represents Arkansas for three terms.

1933: Frances Perkins becomes the first female cabinet member in United States history, after President Franklin D. Roosevelt appoints her secretary of labor.

1935: Mary McLeod Bethune organizes the National Council of Negro Women as a lobbying coalition for black women's groups, to fight racism and sexism.

1948: Eleanor Roosevelt heads the United Nations Commission on Human Rights and successfully campaigns for the passage of the U.N. Declaration of Human Rights.

1953: Clare Booth Luce, the first woman to serve as a high-ranking diplomatic official, is appointed U.S. ambassador to Italy.

1955: Rosa Parks is arrested for refusing to give up her bus seat to a white woman in Montgomery, Alabama, triggering the start of the modern civil rights movement in America.

1957: The number of men and women voters is approximately equal for the first time.

1961: President John F. Kennedy creates the President's Commission on the Status of Women.

1963: The United States Congress passes the Equal Pay Act, enacting the first federal law to prohibit sexual discrimination in the workplace.

1964: Patsy Mink of Hawaii is the first Asian-American woman elected to the U.S. Congress.

1966: Betty Friedan founds the National Organization for Women, which led the women's liberation movement.

1968: Shirley Chisholm of New York is the first African-American woman elected to the U.S. Congress.

1972: The Equal Rights Act finally passes in the U.S. Senate, due mostly to the lobbying power of the National Organization for Women.

1981: Sandra Day O'Connor is the first woman appointed to the U.S. Supreme Court.

1992: Carole Moseley Braun of Illinois is the first African-American woman elected to the United States Senate. The first Mexican American woman, Lucille Roybal-Allard of California, and the first Puerto Rican woman, Nydia Velazquez of New York, are elected to the House of Representatives.

1993: A family and medical leave bill, designed largely by First Lady Hillary Clinton, is signed into law by President William Jefferson Clinton. Thirty bills concerning women's issues are passed by the 103rd Congress, which has more female members than ever.

2000: Hillary Rodham Clinton becomes the first former First Lady to run for a U.S. Senate seat and win.

ABOUT THE AUTHOR

One of Kathryn Lasky's early memories is going to the polls and into the voting booth with her mother. Lasky's mother, Hortense Falender Lasky, would have been four years younger than Kat Bowen. Kathryn Lasky describes her late mother as "an independent, strong-willed, fiercely democratic woman who believed in women's right not only to vote, but also to manage money and plan families." Hortense Falender Lasky was a lifelong member of the League of Women Voters and Planned Parenthood, and was a founding member of Common Cause. Unlike many women of her generation she graduated from college and was a social worker for six years before she married.

"My mother," says Lasky, "was not exactly on the front lines like Eleanor Bowen, but she worked quietly and effectively for many women's causes. Perhaps the best example in my own family was the equality with which my parents participated in every major decision, whether it was about me and my sister, my father's large and very successful business, the stock market, or family finances."

In terms of writing this book Kathryn Lasky recalled many of the memories that her mother shared with her as a child. One of Hortense Lasky's most vivid memories was a terrible fear that her father, Samuel Falender, would be called up to serve in World War I. Lasky used this real-life memory on which to base Kat Bowen's fear of becoming orphaned in that summer of 1917. She also remembers her parents talking about the great influenza epidemic of 1918. Her late father, Marven Lasky, in particular, had very vivid memories from his youth in Duluth, Minnesota. During the epidemic Marven Lasky's parents sent him as a ten-year-old boy to a logging camp on the Canadian border to escape the ravages of the flu, which were at their worst in the city. Kathryn Lasky's book *Marven of the Great North Woods* (Harcourt Brace, 1997) recounts this story. The book received the National Jewish Book Award.

Lasky says the most challenging part of writing this book, *A Time for Courage: The Diary of Kathleen Bowen,* was depicting the ambivalence that Kat Bowen felt as a fourteen-year-old girl in the year of the picket line. She says, "It's not easy being the child of a parent or parents with noble causes. You want to believe in what your parents believe. On the other hand you're still a kid. You want your mom there for you."

Kathryn Lasky believes that the struggle for women's rights is not over and continues to support the same causes that her mother did.

Lasky is the author of more than forty books for children and adults, including three others in the Dear America series: *A Journey to the New World: The Diary of Remember Patience Whipple,* and NCSS Notable Children's Trade Book in the Field of Social Studies and an American Bookseller Pick of the Lists; *Dreams in the Golden Country: The Diary of Zipporah Feldman, a Jewish Immigrant Girl;* and *Christmas After All: The Great Depression Diary of Minnie Swift.* She has also written two in the Royal Diaries series: *Elizabeth I, The Red Rose of the House of Tudor* and *Marie Antoinette.* Kathryn Lasky won the Newbery Honor for the book *Sugaring Time.*

Acknowledgments

Grateful acknowledgment is made for permission to reprint the following:

Cover Portrait: Culver Pictures.

Cover Background: Library of Congress.

Page 203 (top): Girls at the soda fountain, Brown Brothers.
Page 203 (bottom): President Wilson, Library of Congress
(LC Z62 22737).
Page 204 (top): Sojourner Truth, Library of Congress (LC Z62 119343).
Page 204 (bottom): First Women's Rights meeting, Culver Pictures.
Page 205 (top): Mrs O.H.P. Belmont, Library of Congress
(LC Z62 105290).
Page 205 (bottom): Alice Paul, Library of Congress (LC Z62 119710).
Page 206 (top): Marchers in the rain, Library of Congress, National
Woman's Party Collection.
Page 206 (bottom): Suffragettes vigil, Library of Congress, National
Woman's Party Collection (LC Z6 994).
Page 207 (top): Women being arrested, Brown Brothers.

Page 207 (bottom): Lucy Burns in jail, Corbis.

Page 208 (top): Ambulance drivers, Hulton/Archives.

Page 208 (bottom): Red Cross nurse, Brown Brothers.

Page 209 (top): Women voters, Corbis.

Page 209 (bottom): Map by Heather Saunders.

OTHER BOOKS IN THE DEAR AMERICA SERIES

A Journey to the New World
The Diary of Remember Patience Whipple
by Kathryn Lasky

The Winter of Red Snow
The Revolutionary War Diary of Abigail Jane Stewart
by Kristiana Gregory

When Will This Cruel War Be Over?
The Civil War Diary of Emma Simpson
by Barry Denenberg

A Picture of Freedom
The Diary of Clotee, a Slave Girl
by Patricia McKissack

Across the Wide and Lonesome Prairie
The Oregon Trail Diary of Hattie Campbell
by Kristiana Gregory

So Far from Home
The Diary of Mary Driscoll, an Irish Mill Girl
by Barry Denenberg

I Thought My Soul Would Rise and Fly
The Diary of Patsy, a Freed Girl
by Joyce Hansen

West to a Land of Plenty
The Diary of Teresa Angelino Viscardi
by Jim Murphy

Dreams in the Golden Country
The Diary of Zipporah Feldman
by Kathryn Lasky

A Line in the Sand
The Alamo Diary of Lucinda Lawrence
by Sherry Garland

Standing in the Light
The Diary of Catharine Carey Logan
by Mary Pope Osborne

Voyage on the Great *Titanic*
The Diary of Margaret Ann Brady
by Ellen Emerson White

My Heart Is on the Ground
The Diary of Nannie Little Rose, a Sioux Girl
by Ann Rinaldi

The Great Railroad Race
The Diary of Libby West
by Kristiana Gregory

The Girl Who Chased Away Sorrow
The Diary of Sarah Nita, a Navajo Girl
by Ann Turner

A Light in the Storm
The Civil War Diary of Amelia Martin
by Karen Hesse

A Coal Miner's Bride
The Diary of Anetka Kaminska
by Susan Campbell Bartoletti

Color Me Dark
The Diary of Nellie Lee Love
by Patricia McKissack

One Eye Laughing, the Other Weeping
The Diary of Julie Weiss
by Barry Denenberg

My Secret War
The World War II Diary of Madeline Beck
by Mary Pope Osborne

Valley of the Moon
The Diary of María Rosalia de Milagros
by Sherry Garland

Seeds of Hope
The Gold Rush Diary of Susanna Fairchild
by Kristiana Gregory

Christmas After All
The Great Depression Diary of Minnie Swift
by Kathryn Lasky

My Face to the Wind
The Diary of Sarah Jane Price, a Prairie Teacher
by Jim Murphy

Early Sunday Morning
The Pearl Harbor Diary of Amber Billows
by Barry Denenberg

Where Have All the Flowers Gone?
The Diary of Molly Mackenzie Flaherty
by Ellen Emerson White

While the events described and some of the characters in this book may be based on actual historical events and real people, Kathleen Bowen is a fictional character, created by the author, and her journal and its epilogue are works of fiction.

Copyright © 2001 by Kathryn Lasky.

All rights reserved. Published by Scholastic Inc.
557 Broadway, New York, New York 10012.
DEAR AMERICA®, SCHOLASTIC, and associated logos
are trademarks and/or registered trademarks of Scholastic Inc.

Library of Congress Cataloging-in-Publication Data available.

ISBN 0-590-51141-6;
ISBN 0-439-44571-X (pbk.)

10 9 8 7 6 5 4 3   02 03 04 05 06

The display type was set in Parisian.
The text type in this book was set in Caxton Light.
Book design by Elizabeth B. Parisi
Photo Research by Zoe Moffitt and Martha Davidson

Printed in the U.S.A. 23
First paperback printing, October 2002